NIGHT OF THE SQUAWKER

NIGHT OF THE SQUAWKER

R.L. STINE

SCHOLASTIC INC.

Goosebumps book series created by Parachute Press, Inc.
Copyright © 2023 by Scholastic Inc.

ISBN 978-1-338-75220-5

10 9 8 7 6 5 4 3 2 1   23 24 25 26 27

Printed in the U.S.A.   40
First printing 2023

SLAPPY HERE, EVERYONE.

Welcome to My World.

Yes, it's *SlappyWorld*—you're only *screaming* in it! Hahaha.

Some people think I'm a baaad boy. But that's only because they don't know me. If they knew me better, they'd know that I'm *good*—good and evil! Hahaha.

Nothing is more important to me than family. I always say, the family that screams together, screams together. I know. That doesn't make sense. But do you really want to pick a fight with *me*? Haha.

I had a busy week. My brother came to visit. His name is Sloppy the Dummy.

What is Sloppy like? Well, I was walking down the street with him, and a neighbor said, "Slappy, why are you taking your garbage for a walk?"

You get the idea?

Sloppy is so dirty, he was once kicked out of a pigsty!

He's so smelly, he only exhales. He's afraid to inhale! He gives the word *stink* a bad name! Haha.

I asked him, "Sloppy, why are you standing in that mud puddle?"

1

And he said, "It wasn't a mud puddle until I stood in it."

Finally, I got fed up. I said, "Sloppy, isn't it time for you to take a bath?"

And he said, "Why? Is it a leap year?"

Brothers can be weird. I have a story for you now about a brother. His name is Cooper Klavan. In the story, Cooper gets more and more worried about his sister, Anna. You will soon find out that he has *good reason* to be worried.

The story is called *Night of the Squawker.* Believe me, Cooper had a lot to squawk about! Haha.

I'll let Cooper tell it to you.

It's just one more frightening tale from *SlappyWorld!*

"Is that a snake?"

I hiccupped and jumped back. The sticks and twigs I was carrying fell from my hands.

Denzel laughed. "It's not a snake, Coop. It's a weed."

I squinted down at it. "Well, why does it look so much like a snake?" I demanded.

"Maybe it's a snakeweed," my friend replied.

"You're making that up," I muttered. He's always making things up.

Denzel snickered. "I won't tell anyone that Cooper Klavan is afraid of weeds."

I gave him a shove. "I'm not afraid of weeds. I'm afraid of snakes."

He laughed again. "And weeds that look like snakes."

"I'm afraid of big bugs, too," I said. "Bugs that make a loud buzzing sound in your ear."

Denzel made an annoying buzzing sound in my ear. Sometimes he isn't as funny as he thinks he is. He shifted the firewood in his arms. "How much wood do we need?"

"Enough for a very big fire," I said.

I bent down and started to pick up the sticks and twigs I'd dropped.

"We should have brought a wheelbarrow or something," Denzel said. "We can't carry enough wood to keep a fire going all night."

The sun was already lowering behind the trees. Long purple shadows stretched over the ground. A cool breeze made the leaves shiver.

"We'll make a bunch of trips," I said. "We can't let the fire go out."

I picked up a stubby log and added it to the pile of wood in my arms. "Hey—" I cried out when I heard a sound nearby. Soft thuds in the dirt.

Denzel heard it, too. He squinted into the shadows of the trees, holding his breath. We both froze for a few seconds.

"What was that?" I whispered.

Denzel shrugged. "Maybe a raccoon."

I waited for my heart to stop pounding in my chest. "Whatever it was, it stopped," I said. "Let's go to the camp and get the fire started. Then we can come back for more firewood."

"Sounds like a plan," Denzel said. He pointed. "Hey, Coop—there are ants crawling around on that log. You're not afraid of ants, are you?"

"No," I said. "Not unless they start to buzz in my ears."

Denzel groaned. "We're going to need a lot more firewood."

I frowned at him. "Tell me something I *don't* know. The fire has to be big and really tall."

"And we can't let it go out, right?" Denzel said.

"We can't let it go out," I replied. "It's our only chance of keeping the zombies away."

4

2

We walked on in silence for a while, stepping over low shrubs, trying to make our own path through the tangle of trees. Somewhere in the near distance, a bird uttered a long, mournful cry. It was the only sound except for the scrape of our shoes over the carpet of dead leaves on the ground.

"Are we in real trouble?" Denzel asked. His voice came out high and a little shaky.

I shifted the firewood in my arms and kept walking. "Maybe," I answered. "But don't start getting afraid because you'll make *me* afraid."

"We . . . we could get lucky," he stammered.

I nodded. "Maybe the fire will keep us alive until we can get help," I said.

I stumbled over a large round stone and nearly dropped the firewood again.

"Why?" Denzel murmured, staring straight ahead.

"Why what?" I asked.

"Why didn't we listen to everyone? Why didn't we believe them when they said there were zombies—?"

I opened my mouth to answer but stopped with a loud gasp and stumbled into Denzel. We both struggled to stay on our feet as we stared through the trees at a small clearing up ahead.

I heard a low grunt. The sound made my breath catch in my throat. Another grunt.

Squinting hard, I saw dirt fly up from the ground. A big handful, as if it had been tossed into the air.

A wave of panic swept over me. I let the wood fall from my arms and grabbed Denzel's shoulder.

The sunlight shifted and the clearing grew brighter, as if a spotlight was suddenly shining over it.

And now I saw clearly what was happening.

I saw the hands pawing their way up from under the dirt. Two ragged figures tossing dirt, pulling themselves up from a deep rut in the ground. Grunting and moaning as they climbed up from their graves.

"The z-zombies," I stammered.

"Oh no. They're really real," Denzel said. "And they see us."

The skin on their faces hung in dark patches of decay. Their eye sockets were deep and black. They raised themselves up from their graves, first on their knees. Then they stood, arms out at their sides as they caught their balance.

I wanted to run, but fear froze me in place.

I held on to Denzel's trembling shoulder as the two zombies moved toward us, staggering on rubbery legs. They dragged themselves over the dirt, walking side by side as they headed in a straight line for us.

I tried to scream, but no sound came out.

My whole body trembling, I took a step back.

And then one of the zombies opened his mouth in a startled groan as he tripped over a tree root and fell flat on his stomach in the dirt. "Oh, wow," he moaned.

The other zombie burst out laughing. "Ezra, you klutz!"

"Cut! Cut!" I heard Marla Magee shout behind us. Marla was filming the scene on her phone. She ran up to Denzel and me. "Cut! Cut!"

7

"My bad!" Ezra Stone, the clumsy zombie, called out. "Sorry! My sneaker was untied."

Jermaine Miller, the other zombie, picked Ezra up from the dirt.

"I think we have to do the whole scene again," Marla said. "I don't know where I could even edit it."

"I thought it was seriously good," Denzel said. "Until Ezra fell on his face."

I glanced up at the sky. The sun hung even lower behind the trees now. "We've got to work fast," I said. "It's going to be dark soon."

We had been planning the *Zombie Woods* shoot for weeks. Denzel and I wrote the movie script together.

"The next take has to be perfect," I said. "You know we have to hurry. We only have a week, or we'll miss the deadline for the film festival."

"It's not our fault," Ezra said. "It's been raining for days. How were we supposed to shoot in the woods?"

"I wanted to shoot in the rain," Marla said. "That would have been scarier. But you wimps didn't want to get wet."

I rolled my eyes. "Marla, please. We can't start fighting about that now."

She crossed her arms in front of her. "I wasn't starting a fight. I'm just saying."

Marla can be a pain. But she has the newest iPhone with the best camera. And her uncle is on the board of the film festival. Two good reasons to be nice to her.

She waved Ezra and Jermaine back. "Get into

your graves. This time, climb out a little slower. It looked too easy."

"And don't fall down," I said.

Ezra turned and made a face at me. "Duh."

"Whoa. Wait a minute. Don't move," Denzel said. He trotted over to the two zombies.

"What's your problem?" Jermaine asked.

"You're too clean," Denzel said. He picked up a handful of dirt and rubbed it over Jermaine's face. Then he smeared dirt on Ezra's forehead. "You just climbed up from under the ground, remember?"

Ezra rubbed his face. "Maybe we're *clean* zombies."

I groaned. "Can we get started?"

They lowered themselves back into their holes. Denzel and I gathered up the sticks and logs and balanced them in our arms. We backed into the trees to begin the scene again.

Marla raised the phone to her face. "Okay. Action."

Denzel and I began walking, holding on to the firewood as before. Repeating our lines.

"Why?" Denzel said.

"Why what?" I asked.

"Why didn't we listen to everyone? Why didn't we believe them when they said there were zombies—?"

"Well—"

I stopped when I heard a girl's shout from somewhere in the woods.

"Cooper? Cooper? Where *are* you?"

"Cut! Cut!" Marla shouted.

NOW what?

"There you are!"

My sister, Anna, stepped out from the trees. Her coppery hair fell from a green baseball cap turned backward on her head. She wore green denim shorts and a white T-shirt with a yellow banana across the front.

My dad calls her Anna Banana. Anna is eleven. You would think any self-respecting eleven-year-old would *hate* a nickname like that. It makes my teeth itch every time he says it. But she likes it, and she's always wearing this T-shirt with the big banana.

It's not the only weird thing about Anna. But who has time to make a list?

I growled at her. "What are you doing here? You messed up the whole scene."

She glanced around at everyone, then quickly turned back to me. "Dad says you have to come home now. Remember? The fishing trip? It's time to leave."

I let out a long sigh. "Tell Dad you couldn't find me. I don't have time for the fishing trip. Go without me."

Anna spun the cap on her head. "You know if I don't bring you, he'll just come looking for you himself."

Dad's fishing trips are sacred in our family. He and Mom love the outdoors. They love hiking and camping. And Dad is always dragging us on fishing trips to Deepwater Pond, deep in the woods.

If you ask me, the woods are only good for one thing—and that's for making horror movies.

But no one asks me.

"We have to get this movie finished," I told her.

She turned to Ezra and Jermaine, who had climbed out of their holes. "What do you call this film? *Dirty Faces in the Woods*?"

I groaned. "Anna, why do you try to be funny? Can't you face it? You're not funny."

"*I* think she's pretty funny," Marla said.

Who asked her?

Anna stepped up to me and shoved me with both hands. "Cooper, you said I could be in it. Remember?"

I backed away from her. "I'm sorry. I don't have a part for you."

She waved a hand at Ezra and Jermaine. "I could be another zombie. Really. Just put dirt on my face."

I shook my head. "We don't need three zombies, Anna. That's too many."

"Who says?" she shot back.

"Maybe we could shoot three zombies," Marla chimed in.

"Can you please stay out of it?" I yelled.

I saw the hurt look on Marla's face, so I quickly apologized. "Sorry. I didn't mean to shout."

Anna squinted her green eyes at me. "If you don't let me be in your movie, I won't let you use Pokey."

Pokey was Anna's three-legged rabbit.

"Oh, come on, Anna," I said. "You promised we could use him. We need him."

Anna has a collection of sick and wounded animals in the garage that she tends to. She says she wants to be a vet when she grows up. She loves caring for animals, and she's very good with them.

Pokey would be perfect for our horror movie. We needed him to play a victim of the zombie attack.

"So can I be a zombie?" Anna said.

"Maybe," I muttered.

She tugged my arm. "You have to come now. You know how Dad is about leaving late."

"Okay, okay. I'm coming," I said. "But his fishing trips are sooo boring."

I admit it. This time I was wrong about that.

This fishing trip wasn't boring at all.

5

I followed Anna out of the woods and back to our house. Dad waved from the driveway. He already had the truck loaded.

His and Mom's special rods poked over the end of the truck bed. He also packs bamboo poles for Anna and me, but we almost never use them. The picnic basket with our dinner rested against the truck cabin. A cooler stood next to it with bait worms and other supplies inside.

The sun had dipped lower behind the trees. The sky had darkened to purple.

This was my parents' favorite time to go to Deepwater Pond. They both loved to watch the shadows stretch over the ground as the sun set. And they loved to see the night creatures appear from their afternoon hiding places.

Mom and Dad are paleontologists. But they don't really study dinosaurs or old fossils. They study animals that are around today and try to trace them back in history as far as they can.

Mainly, they both study birds. They told us that many birds today can be traced all the way back to

13

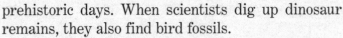

prehistoric days. When scientists dig up dinosaur remains, they also find bird fossils.

I already told you how I feel about the outdoors. I'd rather be inside where it's safe from snakes and insects, playing *Minecraft* with Denzel or writing horror scripts.

But Anna got her love of nature from my parents. The walls of her room are covered with posters of polar bears and penguins and koalas and cute kittens. And "Doctor Anna" is always finding creatures in the woods to nurse back to health.

Mom greeted me by brushing my hair back off my eyes. She's always brushing my hair around, like I'm a dog.

"Where were you?" Dad asked, checking his smart-watch.

"Shooting my video," I said. "You know. My zombie film." I sighed. "It's never going to be finished in time."

Dad adjusted the fishing rods in the truck bed. "Why don't you do a documentary? That would be quicker. Do a documentary about our fishing trip."

I rolled my eyes. "People couldn't take the excitement," I said.

Mom laughed. "Since when are you Mister Sarcastic?"

"Since Dad said I should do a documentary about our fishing trip."

"You're wrong," Dad said. "There's a lot of suspense. Will something happen or not? Will someone catch a fish? Will there be enough sandwiches? Did we remember the mustard? Will we spot a snowy owl after dark?"

"I think I'll stick with zombies," I said.

Dad loves to argue. He talked about his documentary idea all the way to the lake. He knew I'd never do it. But he enjoyed keeping the argument going—even after Mom told him to give me a break.

He stopped the truck at the side of the dirt road that ends at the pond. The shore was soft and grassy, with patches of tall reeds that swayed back and forth in the breeze.

The sky had softened to gray. The sun looked like a dark red ball hanging above the other side of the pond. It made pink and purple ripples in the water.

Mom and Dad started to unload the truck. "Eat first or fish?" Dad asked.

We all knew the answer to that. He always wanted to do some fishing first. We usually ended up eating our sandwiches in the light of the big kerosene camping lantern he always brings.

Anna poked me in the side. "Coop, are those water snakes over there?" she whispered, pointing to the pond.

I wasn't going to fall for that. Anna tries to make me jump every time we visit the pond. "Why don't you run over and find out?" I asked.

Dad handed a fishing rod to Mom. He turned to me. "You should start recording your documentary now," he said. "You don't want to miss anything."

Anna grabbed my arm. "You said I could be in your film. Can I be in the documentary?"

I frowned at her. "You're joking, right? I'm not doing a documentary."

Dad attached a large bait worm to his hook. "Coop, you're making a big mistake."

I turned to Anna. "Which would you rather watch? A horror movie about zombies, or a video about fishing in a pond at night?"

"Fishing in a pond," she said.

She's impossible.

Mom's boots sloshed into the pond. "Do you want your fishing poles?" she asked.

Anna shook her head. "I'm going to take a walk. See if I find that raccoon family from last time."

"Don't go too far," Mom said.

Dad followed her into the water. He turned back to me. "If Anna is going for a walk, I guess you know your job."

"Try to lose her?" I said.

"Ha!" Dad replied. "Love your sense of humor." He pulled his rod back and cast the line out into the pond. "Keep close, Coop. You know how she wanders off. It's going to be dark soon."

"No worries," I said. "Anna, wait for me. Which path are you going to take?"

I squinted into the dim gray light. "Anna?" I called. "Hey, Anna? Anna, where'd you go?"

Of course, Anna didn't answer.

She couldn't have gotten far. But she loves to make me sweat.

There are two dirt paths we usually take. One leads around the shore of the pond. The other path leads into the woods.

Squinting into the gray light, my gaze followed the path around the pond. No sign of her. So I turned and headed into the trees.

Behind me, I heard splashes as Mom and Dad cast their lines into the water. Dad was saying something to Mom, too soft for me to make out the words.

"Hey, Anna?" I tried calling again.

No answer. The only sound was the shuffling of my shoes in the dirt as I hurried along the path and the whisper of leaves overhead.

"Anna? Give me a break. Wait for me!"

The path turned into a long patch of tall trees. Their branches blocked out the sky, making it as black as a tunnel.

I stopped when I heard a soft cry. Was that an animal? Or a person?

I listened hard. The cry was answered by another cry. Now it sounded like two cats calling to each other.

A loud flapping close over my head made me duck. In the darkness, I saw a large bird take off from a low branch. I felt the wind off its wings on the back of my neck. It sent a shiver down my spine.

"Anna! This isn't funny!" I shouted. "You know I'm supposed to watch you. Where are you?"

Silence.

I started to jog. I tried to stay calm. *She couldn't have gotten too far*, I told myself. *She has to be close by.* My shoes sent clumps of dirt flying as I trotted along the path.

"Whoa!" I let out a cry as I fought to keep my balance.

What did my shoe just trip over? A snake?

Another chill made my body shudder.

I struggled to catch my breath as I squinted into the darkness. And then I gasped when I heard Anna's frightened cries.

"Help me! Cooper—help! Help me!"

I stumbled toward Anna's voice.

The path turned, and I saw her in a small, grassy clearing. She was on her knees, bending over a shadowy creature.

"Anna—are you okay?" I cried.

She didn't turn around. "I need help," she said. "This bird—"

As I ran closer, I saw that it was a big, plump bird, nearly as big as a turkey. Its body was covered with long, scraggly feathers. It had a narrow face, dark like a crow, and a long, curled beak. A hoarse honking sound kept bursting from its throat.

"He needs help," Anna said. "Get Mom and Dad. We have to do something."

"Huh? What kind of bird *is* that?" I cried. "He's so big and ugly. And why is he making that awful sound?"

"Because he's in pain," Anna replied. "Look. He hops. I think his leg is broken."

The bird squawked and then hopped a few times, as if showing me his problem.

"Anna, you'd better back away," I said. "That bird is so big—and he looks mean."

"He isn't mean. He's hurt," Anna said. "Go get Mom and Dad. We have to take the bird home and help him."

"But—but—" I started to argue with her. But what was the point?

Once Anna got an idea in her head, there was no way to get it out. I don't think I've ever seen her change her mind.

The bird tossed back his head and started to bleat like a sheep.

"You've already got two sick birds in the garage," I said, shouting over the noise.

"I have an extra cage," Anna said. "Hurry, Cooper. We have to get him in the truck."

"Mom and Dad aren't going to be happy," I told her. "They just started fishing and—"

"What's going on here?" a voice called.

I spun around as Mom and Dad stepped into the clearing. They carried their fishing rods at their sides. Their wet boots gleamed under the rising moonlight.

"We heard yelling," Mom said.

"What *is* that?" Dad cried.

"Anna thinks it's a bird," I said. "But really—"

"Of course it's a bird," Mom said, stepping closer to it. "Why is he on the ground? He seems to be favoring one leg."

"Because he's hurt," Anna said. "Look. I think his leg is broken."

The bird let out more loud, ugly squawks.

Mom bent over to see him better. "Yes. I think you're right." She turned to Dad. "Any idea what kind of bird this is?"

Dad shook his head. "I'd have to look it up. He might be some kind of pheasant. Don't know how he got in these woods."

Anna climbed to her feet. "Well, help me pick him up," she said. "We have to take him home. Maybe we can put a splint on his leg."

I cried out as the bird shot his head toward Anna and snapped his beak. "Look out!" I stumbled back a few steps.

Mom and Dad shook their heads. "Cooper, he's not an alligator. He's only a bird," Mom said.

"You don't have to be afraid of *everything* outdoors," Dad said.

"They make horror movies about birds like this," I said, my eyes still locked on the creature.

Dad moved forward and reached down to lift up the bird. But he shuffled away from Dad's grasp. He tried again, and again the bird dodged to the side.

Dad turned to Anna. "Try to hold him down. Grab his body. And I'll pick him up."

"Okay." Anna moved in front of the bird. She lowered her hands to the bird's back.

Her scream made me gasp.

"OWWWW! OUCH! He BIT me!"

Anna grabbed her arm. "Oww."

The bird uttered a squawk and darted between Anna and my dad. He lowered his dark head and came limping toward me, snapping his beak.

"NO! Hey—NO!" I cried.

I threw myself off the path, staggering sideways over clumps of tall grass. Dad let his fishing rod fall, and he scooped the bird up in his arms.

The bird squawked angrily and tried to bite Dad. But Dad held him tightly in front of his chest.

"Let's see your arm," Mom said to Anna. She raised Anna's arm close. "There's a little mark, but the skin isn't broken."

"It stings," Anna said. "But the bird didn't mean it. He was just frightened."

"He meant it," I said, keeping far away from the creature in Dad's arms. "Didn't you see the look on his face? He meant it."

Dad shook his head. "Give us a break, Cooper." Holding the bird tightly, he began walking out of the clearing to our truck.

Mom and Anna followed close behind him. Anna

kept rubbing her arm. I lingered back, just in case the bird got loose.

"You totally blew it, Coop," Dad said. "I told you to record a documentary of our fishing trip. It turned out to be pretty dramatic, didn't it?" He raised the bird toward me. "Wouldn't this make a good film?"

"No," I said. "No one wants to see an ugly giant bird bite my sister."

Dad kept talking about his video idea. He never likes to let an argument drop.

I slowed down and let the others walk farther ahead. A silvery full moon was high in the sky now. The trees all around us were black against the purple sky.

I stopped when I saw a chain-link fence on the other side of the dirt path. *Who would build a fence here?* I wondered. And then I noticed the sign attached to the fence.

I walked closer to read it. The words were in heavy black letters.

I called to my family. "Hey—did you see this? Did you see this sign?"

They kept walking. They were too far ahead to hear me.

I turned back to the sign and read the words once again:

EXPERIMENTAL AREA. DO NOT FEED THE BIRDS.

Mom drove the truck home while Dad held the bird in his lap. The bird kept making throaty little chirps and shifting his wings up and down, but he seemed a lot calmer.

Dad lowered the bird into the spare cage in the garage. "You can keep him next to Pokey," he told Anna.

"No way," she said. "Carry him to my room. I want to take special care of him. I don't want him in the garage."

I told you, no one argues with Anna. Dad carried the cage up to her room and set it down on the floor under her bedroom window.

Then I helped him unload the truck. There were two cartons of worms that weren't used because the fishing was interrupted. Dad shoved them into the fridge.

I wanted to call Denzel to talk about our zombie movie. But Mom and Dad said we had to help Anna care for the bird.

"I need warm water," Anna said. "First, I'm going to clean his legs."

"Here. Put these on," Mom said. She handed Anna a pair of blue rubber gloves. "That's so you don't get bitten again."

"He's probably covered in germs," I said. "We'll all probably get some kind of horrible bird virus."

Dad snickered. "Then you can make a horror movie about it," he said.

"It's no joke!" I insisted. "Look at his feathers. They're all raggedy and poking out in every direction. Probably crawling with bugs."

"Do you want to give him a haircut?" Mom asked. She can be a joker, too.

"We should be okay if we wear the rubber gloves when we handle him," Dad said.

He lifted the bird from the cage and held him on the rug. Anna got down on her knees and used a washcloth to dab his legs with warm, soapy water.

The bird kept tilting his head and making gurgling sounds from deep in his throat. His feet clawed at the carpet as if he wanted to escape. But he kept his wings down at his sides and didn't try to bite Anna again.

"I think he likes the warm water," Anna said. She dabbed very gently at the injured leg.

"I think we need to fashion a splint for his leg," Mom said. "What should we use?"

Before anyone could answer, the bird opened his beak in a deafening cry. He shot his wings straight up and escaped Dad's grasp. He leaped away from Anna.

Startled, she toppled backward.

The bird screamed again. With a hard flap of his

wings, he leaped into the air. Darting his head from side to side, he shot up to the ceiling. The wings beat against the ceiling for a few seconds.

I screamed as the bird lowered his head and dive-bombed from the ceiling, swooping down at top speed, his beak wide open, as he aimed right for my throat.

SLAPPY HERE, EVERYONE.

Haha. Cooper shouldn't panic. Maybe the bird is just being friendly.

After all, Cooper forgot to brush his hair that morning. Maybe the bird just thinks he's a *nest*! Hahaha!

Cooper is definitely afraid of the bird. And guess what? He has good reason to be afraid!

I'm not a big fan of birds, either. The only bird I like is the one on the table at Thanksgiving! Hahaha.

Think the bird is going to cause a lot more trouble? Three guesses . . .

10

THUD.

The bird slammed into my chest, knocking me flat on my back.

"Off . . ." I choked out. "Get it OFF me!"

He flapped his wings hard against my face. Smothering me. I tried to push him away with both hands, gasping to breathe.

Finally, I saw Dad's fingers wrap around the bird's heaving body. He lifted the bird off me and held him in his outstretched hands.

Mom chuckled. "Cooper, this is better than any of your horror movie ideas."

"It isn't funny, Mom!" I shouted. I brushed brown feathers off my shirt. My chest still ached. I kept picturing the big creature dive-bombing me from the ceiling.

Dad slid the bird into the cage. "You'll have to be careful with this one, Anna Banana," he said. "I think this guy is going to be a difficult patient."

"He's just frightened," Anna said. "I'll get him calmed down."

"Let's deal with the bad leg first," Mom said. "I

think we can use a Popsicle stick as a splint."

"I'm outta here," I said. My legs were still shaky as I backed out of Anna's room. "I don't care what you say. That bird is scary. I'm sticking to zombies."

The next morning was Saturday. I woke up yawning and still feeling sleepy. The bird had kept me up late. Anna's room is next to mine, and I could hear him chirping and bumping up against his cage all night.

The sky outside my bedroom window was cloudy and gray. Perfect for our zombie video. I texted Denzel and told him to meet me in the woods.

I gulped down my cereal. I wanted to get away without any discussion from Anna. But, of course, that was impossible.

"Hope you didn't have nightmares about the bird," she said, sneering.

I swallowed a chunk of cereal. "How could I have nightmares?" I said. "I didn't sleep all night because the stupid bird kept making noise."

Mom took a long sip from her coffee mug. "Anna, close your door tonight so Cooper can sleep."

"But it gets too stuffy with the door closed," Anna replied.

Everyone in my family likes to argue.

I texted Marla to make sure she was ready. We had so little time to get our movie finished. I hoped we could get a lot done today.

But, of course, nothing ever goes smoothly. At least, not in *my* life.

11

My first problem of the day came at Ezra's house. My zombie actor lives on the next block over. I knew something was wrong when his mom greeted me at the door, shaking her head.

"So sorry, Coop," she said. "I'm afraid I have bad news. Ezra can't come out today. He has an upset stomach."

A zombie with an upset stomach?

Another time I would have thought that was funny. But not today.

"Is he throwing up?" I asked. "That might work for our zombie movie."

She stared at me for a long moment. "I'm sorry. I can't let him out."

So that's how I ended up using Anna as the second zombie.

Believe me, I didn't want to get her involved. I even thought of letting Jermaine be the only zombie. But one zombie isn't a very impressive zombie attack.

So I hurried back home to talk to Anna. I found her in her room. Mom was holding the bird down with both hands, and Anna was wrapping tape around his injured leg.

Mom looked up when I walked in. "We have a real difficult patient here," she said.

"I know how to solve the problem," I said.

They both looked at me. "How?"

"Open the window and let him fly out."

Anna let out an angry cry. Mom shook her head at me. "Cooper, don't be cruel. You know your sister likes to care for these animals."

I turned to Anna. "Ezra is sick. I need you for my video. You can be the second zombie."

Anna thought about it for a moment. "Sorry. I have other plans," she said.

"Huh? Excuse me?" I said. "Yesterday, you *begged* me—"

"That was yesterday," she replied. She petted the bird's back. Her fingers slid through its thick brown and gray feathers. "I have to stay home and take care of Oggie."

"Oggie?" I cried. "You gave him a name?"

Of course she gave him a name!

I didn't wait for her to answer. "I need you more than that stupid bird does," I said. "Come on, Anna. You have to do it."

A sly grin crossed her face. "Do I get paid?"

My mouth dropped open. "Paid? Uh . . . okay. I'll give you this week's allowance."

Her grin faded. "You don't get an allowance, remember?"

"Anna, stop being difficult," Mom said. "You know you want to be in Coop's video."

31

Thank you, Mom.

Anna kept running her hand back through the bird's feathers. He stood quietly now. He seemed to like it.

"Okay, okay," she said finally. "But I don't want to be the second zombie."

I curled my fists into tight balls. "What *do* you want to be?" I demanded.

"I want to be the *first* zombie."

"Fine," I said. "Whatever. You can work it out with Jermaine. But let's go. Hurry. Everyone is waiting in the woods."

Marla and Denzel turned Anna into a zombie. Denzel rubbed dead leaves on her T-shirt and ripped one of the sleeves. Marla spread dirt over Anna's face and added a few chunks of soil to her hair.

"Where do we start?" Jermaine asked. He stood in the grave we had dug for the two zombies.

"We have to start the scene at the beginning," Marla said. "Especially since we have a new zombie."

Denzel and I began to collect firewood to carry in our arms. "Anna, get in the hole with Jermaine," I told her. "When Marla gives the signal, you two zombies slowly climb up from under the ground."

No reply.

I glanced around. "Anna? Hey—where'd you go?"

"Whoa!" Denzel uttered a startled cry. Jermaine and Marla turned to stare.

Anna was squatting down near the ground. Her head was bobbing up and down—*and she was pecking at the dirt like a bird!*

12

"Anna!" I let out a cry and went running over to her. "Anna—what are you doing?"

I grabbed her by the shoulders and pulled her up. Finally, she stopped pecking at the grass and raised her eyes to me. "What are you doing?" I repeated.

She blinked a few times. "Doing? I wasn't doing anything."

I held on to her shoulders. "Yes, you were," I said. "We all saw you. You were bobbing your head like a bird and pecking the ground."

Anna laughed. "No, I wasn't."

Denzel stepped up beside me. "We saw you," he said. "Was that some kind of joke?"

She squinted up at him. "A joke? What's your problem, Denzel? I wasn't doing anything."

Marla stepped in front of us, holding her iPhone. "Can we move on?" she asked. "We have to shoot the scene. I think it's going to rain."

"Come on," I said. I pulled Anna to her feet. "You and Jermaine get down in the grave. Denzel and I are going to come walking by with our firewood." I studied her. "Are you okay?"

She pulled free of my hand. "Sure. I'm fine, Coop. Give me a break."

Then she tossed back her head and let out a long, loud rooster crow to the sky.

Marla started toward her. But I raised a hand to stop her. "Just ignore her," I told Marla. "Don't pay any attention. Anna thinks she's being funny."

"No, I don't," Anna said.

Jermaine grabbed Anna's hand and helped her down beside him in the grave. Denzel loaded our arms with firewood. Marla raised her phone and yelled, "Action!" And we started the scene.

"Coop, do you want pepperoni or plain?" Mom asked.

I peered at the two open pizza boxes at the end of the table. "You know I always want pepperoni, Mom," I said. "Why do you ask me every time?"

"To give you a choice," Mom said. She slid a pepperoni slice onto a plate and Anna passed it down to me.

"Don't turn pizza into an argument," Dad said.

"I'm not arguing," I said.

Anna had already started her plain slice. She hadn't washed up. She still had smears of dirt on her face from the afternoon shoot.

Dad passed her the salad bowl.

"I don't want salad," she said. "I just want pizza."

"Don't turn salad into an argument," Dad told her.

She took the bowl and set it to the side. I knew she'd never eat any of it. In my house, *stubborn* is spelled A-N-N-A.

Mom squinted at Anna's dirty hands. "Anna, get up and go wash your hands."

"I can't. I'm too hungry." She bit off a huge chunk of crust.

"How can you eat with dirty hands like that?"

"Easy."

Mom sighed. "Well? How did the shoot go?"

"Great," Anna answered before I could.

"We had a very good day," I said. "We shot three scenes before it started to rain." I raised my eyes to my sister across the table. "Anna was an awesome zombie."

Dad laughed. "Is that supposed to be a compliment?"

Mom smiled at Anna. "Did you hear that? Your brother just said something nice about you."

Anna didn't smile back. Her eyes were down, and she had stopped eating. She opened her mouth in a low moan.

"Anna? Are you okay?" Mom asked.

Anna slowly shook her head. "I . . . I don't feel very well," she stammered.

"Did you eat your pizza too fast?" Dad said.

She didn't answer him. Just moaned again.

Mom walked up behind her and placed a hand on Anna's forehead. "A little warm," Mom said. "You might be running a low temperature."

"I just feel . . . kinda sick," Anna murmured.

"I hope you didn't catch something in the woods today," Dad said. "Why don't you go up to your room and lie down? Mom and I will come up in a few minutes and check you out."

Anna scraped her chair back and climbed to her feet. We watched her slump out of the kitchen. I heard her start to slowly climb the stairs.

35

"What's that about?" Dad said in a whisper.

Mom shrugged in reply.

I swallowed a chunk of pizza. I could still hear Anna on the stairs.

The three of us were silent for a moment.

And then we all jumped when we heard Anna's scream of horror.

13

We pushed back our chairs, leaped to our feet, and went running to the front stairs. I got there first. I saw Anna halfway up, her mouth hanging open, pointing frantically at something on the next step.

"Help! Help me!" Anna shrieked.

She was pointing at Suzie, her orange tabby cat. Suzie was curled up on the stairs, staring at Anna with her green eyes.

Dad uttered a cry of surprise. "Anna? What's wrong?"

"Get her away from me!" Anna screamed. "Please—help! Get that cat away from me!"

My heart was pounding. I felt too confused to move.

"Anna, why are you screaming about your cat?" Mom demanded.

Anna kept pointing down at Suzie, her whole body trembling. "P-please—do something! Get her away from me!"

Dad climbed the stairs and lifted Suzie with one hand. Then he backed down the stairs with her.

Anna stood gripping the banister, her eyes on the cat.

"Suzie has always been your cat," Mom said. "How can you suddenly be terrified of her?"

Anna blinked a few times. "I . . . I don't know," she murmured. Then she turned and ran up the stairs to her room.

No way I could get to sleep that night.

For one thing, I was worried about Anna. She was always a little moody and strange—but not *this* strange.

I kept picturing her bent over, pecking the ground in the woods this afternoon. And I couldn't stop thinking about her screaming her head off, terrified of her own cat.

Mom thought she may have caught something in the woods. She wanted to take her to a doctor right away.

Of course, Dad had to argue. "Wait till morning," he said. "I took her temperature. It was normal. Let's see how she feels tomorrow."

They argued about it for a while. Then, I guess Dad won because Anna stayed in her bed and went to sleep.

Now it was after midnight, and I was tossing and turning, thinking about the day. I thought about my zombie movie. If Anna was okay, we could probably finish shooting it tomorrow. But if she was sick . . .

The bird in Anna's room next door was squawking his head off. I wrapped my pillow over my head, trying to block out the horrible screeches. *He's going to wake up the whole house,* I thought.

It's the middle of the night. Why can't that bird shut up?

I shut my eyes as hard as I could. I tried humming to myself to drown out the bird squawks. I buried myself under the covers.

Nothing worked. The hoarse bleats and squawks came from the other side of the wall. I knew the noises would keep me up all night—unless I did something.

Holding my ears, I sat up and thought. It didn't take long to come up with a plan. I crossed the room to my closet and tugged out the extra wool blanket for my bed.

"Maybe a blanket over his cage will make the bird go to sleep," I told myself.

Carrying the bundled-up blanket in my arms, I tiptoed out of my room. The bird squawks were even louder out in the hall. I was surprised Mom and Dad couldn't hear them from downstairs.

I stopped outside Anna's door. I didn't want to wake her. I just wanted to slip into the room and cover the birdcage with the blanket.

Carefully, I turned the knob and pushed the door open. The room was dark except for a pale cone of silvery moonlight from the window.

I shuffled silently toward the cage on the floor. Halfway there, I stopped.

"Oh." I let out a soft cry and nearly dropped the blanket.

The cage—it was empty.

I squinted into the pale light. The cage door stood wide open. The bird was out.

I heard a squawk. I spun around.

And saw the bird—*flying right at Anna's head.*

14

I opened my mouth in a startled scream.

The bird fluttered over Anna's face. Anna sighed but didn't wake up.

"Anna— Hey, Anna—!" I cried.

She groaned and opened one eye.

I gasped as the ceiling light flashed on and the room filled with bright yellow light. Mom and Dad were at the door. They burst into the room in their pajamas.

"Cooper—why are you screaming?" Dad asked.

"What on earth—" Mom started. Then she saw the bird. He had landed on Anna's head and stood there facing us.

"Mmmmm?" Anna woke up slowly. She raised her head off the pillow. The bird rode up with her. He spread his claws on her forehead and opened his wings as if preparing to fight.

"Is this *happening*?" Mom demanded in a whisper. Her voice was still clogged from sleep. "How did the bird—"

Dad waved his hands as he carefully stepped toward Anna's bed, one inch at a time. "Stay calm, everyone. I've got this."

The bird arched his head stiffly as Dad crept slowly toward the bed.

"I . . . I think Oggie is just trying to protect me," Anna said softly.

"Maybe he thinks your head is an egg!" I said from the doorway.

"Cooper, shut up!" Anna snapped.

"Shhh." Dad gestured with both hands again. He took a step, then another. And wrapped his hands around the bird's middle.

The bird let out a squawk. Then he went limp.

Dad carried him to the cage. Slid him inside. And carefully bolted the cage door shut.

"Whew." I let out a long sigh of relief. Anna was safe.

"That door never stayed shut," Dad said. "I'll try to fix it in the morning."

Anna sat on the edge of the bed, rubbing her forehead.

Mom hurried over to her. "Are you okay?"

"Yes. Fine," Anna said. She shook her head. "That was a little weird."

"It was majorly weird," I said, finally starting to relax and feel normal again.

Dad turned to me. "Coop, what were you doing in Anna's room?"

"I . . . well . . . I was going to put a blanket over the bird's cage," I said. "He was making such a racket, I couldn't get to sleep."

"Strange," Anna said, staring at me. "I didn't hear anything."

She stretched her hands above her head and yawned. "I had the weirdest dream."

"What was it?" Mom asked.

"I was flying," Anna said. "Flying high in the sky over the woods. I could see all the green trees beneath me. I flew right into a flock of birds. There must have been dozens of them. A thick flock. I flew right into them and I just kept flying."

"Then what happened?" I asked.

Anna shrugged. "Then you woke me up. That was the end of the dream."

"It's not so weird," Mom said, tucking the blanket back over her. "You had a bird on your head, so you dreamed about birds."

"I guess," Anna said. She yawned again and settled her head down on her pillow.

"The excitement is over," Dad said, leading Mom to the door. "No more squawks and no more screams, okay? I need my beauty sleep." He and Mom vanished into the hall and down the stairs to their room.

I took one last glance at the bird. He stood stiffly at the front of his cage, staring out at me. At least he had stopped squawking.

"G'night," I muttered to Anna. I started to the door, ready to turn off the light, but I stopped.

I saw Anna reach under the covers. She was plucking at something under the sheet. When she pulled her hands up, they held a bunch of long brown feathers.

Whoa. Hold on, I thought. *If the bird was sitting on her head, how did the feathers get under the covers?*

43

15

I kept yawning at breakfast the next morning. I felt as if I hadn't gotten any sleep at all.

Anna was her usual grumpy self. "Why can't I have orange juice or apple juice like every other kid in America?" she whined. "Why do I have to have this weird juice Dad mixes every morning?"

"It isn't weird," Dad said, rolling his eyes. "It's my special Power Juice. Pear juice and grapefruit juice and some vitamins. It's better for you."

"And no pulp," I said, finishing my glass. "I hate pulp."

"Can't we have a peaceful morning and not argue about my Power Juice?" Dad said.

Mom had a skillet sizzling on the stove. "A real breakfast this morning," she said. She carried a plate to the table and started to put it down in front of Anna. "This will cheer you up, Anna. I made your favorite. Fried eggs on toast with grape jelly."

"Oh, yuck!" Anna made a disgusted face. "No! Take it away! No eggs!"

"But, Anna—" Mom started.

Anna shoved the plate away. She nearly knocked

it out of Mom's hands. "No eggs! I *hate* eggs!"

Dad was sitting at the end of the table, still in his pajamas. He jumped to his feet. "Hold on, Anna Banana," he said. "What is your problem? Eggs were always your favorite breakfast. You're always begging us for eggs."

"I can't stand them!" Anna cried. "I'm going to be sick. Seriously." She lowered her head. Her face suddenly looked kind of green. Her stomach started to make rumbling sounds. I could hear the gurgling all the way across the table.

Mom stood confused, holding the plate above the table.

"I'll take them," I said, and reached for the plate. "I like eggs, too, you know. I don't know what's up with Anna, but—"

Anna held her hand over her mouth. "Do you have to eat those so close to me? It's literally making me sick."

"I'll try to eat fast," I said. I swallowed a chunk of egg and toast. "It sure is good." I raised the egg on the toast toward her.

"Don't torture your sister," Dad said. "She's definitely in a weird mood."

"No, I'm not," Anna said.

Mom stood at the kitchen counter. "I'll get you cereal for breakfast," she told Anna. She started for the cabinet door—then stopped.

"What's wrong?" Dad asked her.

"I could swear I left four more eggs on the counter," Mom said. "But there are only three here." She took a step back and peered down at the floor. "Did one of them roll away?"

Dad walked over to help her look for it. "I didn't hear anything fall and crack," he said.

"The only thing that's cracked is Anna's head," I chimed in.

"Shut up, Coop," Anna snapped.

Dad raised his pointer finger to me. "No jokes."

"Who's joking?" I said. I went back to my eggs on toast. They tasted so awesome with grape jelly.

"Well, that's a mystery about the missing egg," Mom said. She poured Anna a bowl of Frosted Flakes and carried it to the table. Then she sat down at her place and raised her coffee mug.

"I'm enjoying Anna's eggs," I said. I reached for my juice and accidentally sent my fork tumbling to the floor.

"At least you're not a klutz," Anna muttered.

I slid off the chair and ducked under the table to get the fork. And that's when I saw something strange.

Back in my chair, I motioned to my sister. "Anna, stand up for a minute."

"Excuse me?"

"Don't argue," I said. "Just stand up."

She made a disgusted face, slid her chair back, and slowly stood up.

I pointed to her chair. "Look. Anna was sitting on the egg."

Mom choked on her coffee. Dad made a startled gurgle in his throat.

We were all standing now, gazing at the egg on Anna's chair.

Anna shook her head. "How did *that* get there?"

46

"She was sitting crooked. She was sitting on the missing egg," I told my parents. I squinted at Anna. "What were you doing? Trying to hatch it?"

That made Mom and Dad laugh. But it wasn't funny.

What was happening to Anna?

16

After breakfast, I peered out the kitchen window. The sky was gray with dark storm clouds hanging low. So I hoped we could finish the zombie video before the rain came.

I hurried upstairs to change my clothes. But on the way to my room, I had an idea.

Anna was still downstairs. I grabbed my phone and stepped into her room. The bird stood quietly in his cage. His brown-and-gray head poked out through the cage bars.

"So you're quiet this morning," I said to him. He stared out at me but didn't reply. "Maybe you're some kind of night bird," I said.

What kind of bird *was* he? Mom and Dad said they didn't know. I was determined to find out.

I dropped to my knees in front of the cage and snapped a bunch of photos of him. Then I went back to my room and started to study bird photos on my laptop.

I didn't find a match. But I did find an app called Feathered Finder. It was a bird-identifying app. You upload a photo of a bird, and it tells you what kind of bird it is.

My dad uses an app like that, but for fish. Sometimes he can't identify the fish he's caught. So he finds it on the fish app.

Humming to myself, I uploaded my best photo of Oggie to the app. Then I waited for the answer to pop up on the screen.

I thought it would happen instantly. But the app was taking a lot of time. Then, finally, a message appeared beneath my photo: *Not recognized.*

Maybe a better photo will work, I told myself.

So I tried a different photo. After a long wait, the same message appeared: *Not recognized.*

"Weird," I muttered. I stared at the photo. "Are you some kind of Martian bird no one has ever seen before?"

My parents work from home. I hurried down to their office at the back of the house. They don't like to be interrupted when they're working. But I had to tell them what I had just learned.

They both looked up from their laptops as I stepped up to their side-by-side desks. "Cooper, what's up?" Mom asked. "I thought you were heading to the woods."

"I am," I said. "But I have something I want to tell you." I told them the whole story of the bird app and how it couldn't identify Anna's bird. And I told them how I was worried about Anna. How ever since the bird bit her, she was acting weird. I spilled it all without taking a breath. When I finished, I was breathing hard.

Dad placed a hand on my shoulder. "Cooper, breathe," he said. "Calm down. We know you're worried about Anna. But—"

"There are *thousands* of bird species in the world," Mom interrupted. "Actually, there are over *ten thousand* different species of birds. Believe it or not, some of them even trace all the way back to pre-historic times."

"I know, but—" I started.

"So there's no way an app can identify every species," Mom said. "There are just too many of them!"

"We'll take a look at our reference books," Dad said. "I'm sure we can find an answer for you."

"But you have to stop worrying," Mom said. "That bird is just another creature Anna wants to help."

I took a deep breath. "But . . . b-b-but haven't you noticed?" I stammered. "Haven't you noticed how strange Anna has been acting?"

They both narrowed their eyes at me. "You mean about being afraid of her cat and not wanting to eat eggs?" Mom asked.

I nodded. "Yes. Aren't you worried about that?"

"She's just going through a phase," Dad said.

What does that mean?

Why do parents like to say that?

I mean, what's a phase *anyway?*

Whatever it meant, I didn't think Anna was going through one. But I didn't have time to get into another one of their arguments.

Instead, I went back upstairs so Anna and I could get ready for the woods. "Be sure to wear the same clothes you wore yesterday," I told her.

"But they're all covered in dirt," she replied.

"That's the point. They have to match yesterday's shoot," I said.

50

"Do I get any lines today?" she demanded. "Do I get to say anything?"

"Of course not," I said. "You're a zombie. You just growl and grunt. Think you can handle it?"

She stuck her tongue out at me. "Coop, you owe me big-time for helping you out."

"You're joking," I said. "You asked me to be in the video, so I decided to give you a break."

We could have argued all morning. But who had time? I had to get in touch with everyone and tell them where to meet us.

In my room, I changed into the same T-shirt and dirt-covered jeans I had worn yesterday. Then I grabbed my phone and began to text everyone.

I called Marla because I wanted to describe what the shots should be. But it was impossible to talk. In the next room, the bird started squawking again. I could barely hear Marla.

"Wait," I told her. "I'll call you right back."

I crossed the room to the hall. "Anna, can't you make that bird stop squawking?" I called.

I don't think she heard me. The bird cries were too loud.

I stepped up to my sister's room and peered in through the open door. "Anna—?"

I stopped and stared. The bird was huddled on the floor of his cage, sound asleep.

And Anna was sitting cross-legged on the rug, her face raised to the window, chirping and squawking her head off.

17

I froze in shock. I don't know how long I stood there, watching her chirp at the sky. A hundred thoughts flashed through my mind, all of them confused. I actually felt dizzy.

But then my mind suddenly cleared and an idea began to form.

Silently, I raised my phone. I turned it to video and pressed RECORD.

I ducked back as far as I could in the doorway so Anna wouldn't see me. I held the phone steady in front of me. I didn't take a breath. I didn't want it to show up in the sound.

Anna chirped away. Her song turned sweet, like a happy canary. And as I watched and recorded, she raised one arm and ducked her head under it.

She was preening herself like a bird!

This was too unbelievable. I began shaking with excitement and fear, shaking too hard to keep the video still.

I'd been holding my breath for too long! So I pushed STOP on the phone and let out a long whoosh of air. I tiptoed back to my room and closed my door carefully. Then I threw myself on the bed.

This is too much!

This can't be happening!

Why is Anna acting like a bird?

Should I tell Mom and Dad?

Anna was definitely going through a phase. But it was a frightening phase they should know about.

My phone beeped. A text from Denzel:

Where r u? We're all waiting.

"I'll figure this out later," I told myself. I tucked the phone into my jeans and hurried back to Anna's room.

She was standing up now, holding something in her fist. When I burst into the room, she swept the fist behind her back so I wouldn't see.

But I glimpsed it clearly before she tried to hide her hand. She was holding a bunch of brown and gray feathers between her fingers.

"What do you want?" she demanded.

"It's time to go. Everyone is there already," I said.

"Okay, I'm coming. Give me a minute."

I backed up and waited in the hall. I gave her a chance to get rid of the feathers.

Was I nervous and confused and a little scared about what was happening to her?

That's one way to put it.

I wanted to grab her and shake her and say, "Anna, what's happening? Why are you doing those bird things? Do you feel strange? Tell me!"

But I didn't want to frighten her.

I tried to hint about it as we walked to the woods. "Anna, how ya doing?"

She squinted at me. "Okay. Why are you asking me that?"

"No reason. I just asked how ya doing."

She kept her suspicious gaze on me. "You never asked me that question before, Cooper."

"Oh, please," I moaned. "Please don't start an argument because I asked how you were doing."

She hurried ahead of me. I had to trot to catch up. "I heard that bird squawking his head off again this morning," I said.

Only it wasn't the bird—it was YOU!

"Seriously?" She kept her eyes straight ahead. "I didn't hear him."

"You were in your room and you didn't hear the chirping? It sounded like *ten* birds in there!" I said.

She shrugged. "You're hearing things. Maybe you should get your ears cleaned."

"Not funny," I said.

We stepped onto the path that led into the trees. "You need dirt," I said, changing the subject. "Marla will have to work on your face."

"But who's going to work on *yours*?" she snapped. Then she burst out laughing at her own joke.

Between the trees, I could see the stone pile where we had all agreed to meet. It was a low hill of smooth, white stones in a small clearing.

Jermaine jumped up from his perch on the stones and waved as we entered the clearing.

Denzel came running up to us. "What's up? We couldn't start till you got here."

"I . . . was waiting for Anna," I said.

"Liar!" She slapped my shoulder. "I didn't keep you waiting."

Yes, you did. I had to wait while you were preening yourself and chirping like a bird.

Marla walked over and took Anna by the arm. She patted Anna's face. "There's some good mud over here," she said. "Let's get you zombified."

Denzel waved a script in his hand. "Are we sticking to this? Are we keeping the scene as it is?" he asked me.

I nodded. "You and I are trying to escape from the zombies. We run to this stone hill. We think we might be safe if we climb it. But then stones begin to topple down from the top. We look up, and we see the two zombies coming down the side of the hill after us."

"Pretty cool," Denzel said. "But what if we start to climb the stones? Let's say we make it halfway up—and *then* we see the two zombies staring down at us from the top."

"Good," I said. "That's better. Then you and I are trapped halfway up and halfway down. Let's try it."

I turned and shouted to Marla. "Did you hear that?"

She stepped out from behind a clump of tall reeds. "Hear what?"

"A change of plans," I said. "Denzel had a good idea." I explained it to her.

She glanced around. Then she backed up several steps. "I'll shoot from here. That way I can focus on you and Denzel. Then I can sweep up to the two zombies at the top of the hill."

"Sounds like a plan," Denzel said.

I motioned to Jermaine. "You and Anna need to climb the stones from the other side."

"Then wait for my signal," Marla said. "And the two of you step up to the top of the hill."

"You got it," Jermaine replied. He glanced around. "Where's Anna?"

"Huh?" Marla turned to the tall reeds where she had been working on Anna's zombie face. She cupped her hands around her mouth. "Anna? Hey, Anna? Are you still over there?"

No reply.

"Anna?" I called. "We need you. Where'd you go?"

Silence.

Jermaine's shoes crunched on the stones as he walked to look for her behind the reeds. "She isn't here," he reported.

I spun around. Did she go back to the path? I squinted into the trees. "Anna? Hey, Anna—where *are* you?"

"Oh, wow! I don't *believe* it!"

Denzel's cry made me jump.

"No way!" Denzel shouted.

I turned and saw the startled look on his face. And saw him pointing—pointing straight up.

I tilted my head back—and there she was.

Anna. My sister. Half-hidden in the shadow of leaves. Gazing up at the sky. Perched on a high branch of a tree.

56

18

"Anna! Come down!"

"What are you doing?"

"How? How did you climb up there?"

We were all standing at the bottom of the tree, shouting up to her.

Anna didn't seem to hear us. She squatted on the high branch, gazing up at the sky.

"Anna? Hey—Anna?" I had my hands cupped around my mouth and I shouted at the top of my lungs.

I gasped as the tree branch made a cracking sound and tilted beneath her. But she didn't seem to notice.

I turned and saw that Denzel had his phone out. "We need to get help," he said.

"I already called 911," Marla said. "Someone is coming to bring her down."

Jermaine had his phone out, too. "They have to bring a very tall ladder," he said. "And fast. Do you see that branch bobbing under her weight?"

"I see it," I said. "If only she could hear us . . ."

I raised my phone. I turned it to *video* and began to record. *I might need this*, I thought.

Up on the tree limb, Anna tipped her head to one side and let out a loud *chirp*.

I used the *zoom* function on my phone and got as close as I could. Anna chirped some more. In the phone, I could see she had a smile on her face. She seemed so happy.

Why wasn't she frightened? Why was she up there? Why was she pretending to be a bird?

I stopped the video and slid the phone into my jeans. Then I tried shouting up to her again.

This time she heard me.

She nearly lost her balance as she lowered her head. "Coop?"

I gasped. "Don't move!" I shouted. "We called for help."

Her face twisted in confusion. "Help? Why do I need help?"

I ignored my pounding heart. "Just stay still," I called.

We all huddled under the tree staring up at her. "Anna, how did you get up there?" Denzel demanded.

Anna blinked several times. "Up where?" she replied.

"Up in the tree!" Denzel shouted.

She glanced around, and her mouth dropped open. "I'm ... in a tree?" She grabbed the branch with both hands.

Her body lurched forward, then back.

I shut my eyes. *Don't fall. Please don't fall!*

58

She steadied herself on the limb, gripping it tightly at her sides.

"Don't move—please!" I begged.

"How did I get up here?" Anna called down to us.

"That's what we asked *you*!" Jermaine cried. "How?"

"I . . . I don't know," Anna stammered.

I took a deep breath to steady my heartbeat. "Marla, did you say they're sending the fire department?" I asked. "What's taking them so long?"

"It's only been a few minutes," Marla said.

"How can they get their truck here in the middle of the woods?" Jermaine said.

"That's *their* problem!" I snapped.

"They can carry a ladder along the dirt path," Denzel said. He swallowed. "I hope."

"What did you tell them?" I asked Marla.

"I said a girl was stuck in a tree. They said—"

She stopped because we heard voices approaching. And the heavy thud of running footsteps.

"They're here!" I cried.

Two men in dark gear burst out from the tall reeds at the edge of the clearing. They wore heavy black-and-yellow jackets. One of them had a firefighter's helmet tilted back on his head. The other one was younger, bare-headed, his blond hair down to his shoulders.

The three of us ran to greet them.

"We couldn't drive the truck this far into the woods," the younger one said. "The path is too narrow."

"Someone is up in a tree?" his partner demanded. "Show us!"

"She's up there! My sister!" I ran to the tree.

59

"She's on a high branch," Marla said, trailing after us. "You'll need a ladder."

"Let's see," the older firefighter said. He pointed. "Up there?"

I nodded. "Yes." And then I stepped aside to give them room.

The older one took off his helmet and tilted back his head. They both gazed up to the top of the tree. They stood without moving for a long moment.

"Where?" the younger one asked, still staring up into the leafy branches.

"I don't see her," his partner said, squinting hard. "Point to her. It's very shady up there."

I stepped in front of them and pointed to the high limb. "There. That one," I said. "She—"

I stopped with a gasp and focused on the branch.

The empty branch.

Anna was gone.

19

"Noooo!" I wailed. "Did she fall?"

We all ran behind the tree and studied the blanket of dead leaves on the ground.

No. No sign of her.

"Anna? Can you hear me?" I screamed. "Where *are* you?"

The younger firefighter turned to me. "Is this the right tree?"

"Of *course* it is!" I cried, my voice high and shrill from my panic. I raised my face to the top of the tree. "Anna? Anna? *Answer* me!"

"Why are you shouting?" a voice called.

I spun around so fast, I nearly toppled over. "Anna?"

She came walking slowly from the dirt path behind us. Her hair was wild around her face. But, otherwise, she looked perfectly fine.

I ran over to her and grabbed her by the shoulders. "You—you're okay?" I cried.

"Sure," she said. She gazed up at me, confused. "Why wouldn't I be?"

The two firefighters stepped up to us. "Is this some kind of joke?" the younger one asked.

"It's a serious crime to phone in a false report to 911," his partner said.

They both stared at my sister, frowning, waiting for her answer.

"I didn't call 911," Anna said. She turned to me. "Coop, was it you?"

"Just explain!" I cried. "You were up on that high tree limb. How did you get down?"

Anna blinked a few times. "Tree limb? Me? No, it wasn't me."

"We all saw you," Denzel said. He turned to the two firemen. "She was up on that branch. This isn't a joke."

The older guy scratched his head. "Then how *did* you get down?" he demanded.

"Down from where?" Anna said. "I never went up. I was in the woods."

The firefighters shook their heads. "This is serious—" one of them started.

Marla pushed her way to the center of the group. "We all saw you, Anna," she said. "You were on that high branch." She pointed. "You scared us to death. Don't say you weren't up there. We all saw you clearly."

"How did you get back down? Tell us," Denzel demanded. "We know you didn't fly."

Anna shut her eyes. "Stop. Please stop," she said softly. "You're confusing me."

"You're confusing me, too," the older fireman said. He motioned to his partner. "Let's go, Ernesto." They began to walk to their truck. "Don't do this

62

again. That's a warning," he called back to us without turning around.

We watched them disappear into the trees. Then I spun and studied Anna. "What's that in your hair?" I asked.

I reached into her hair and plucked out two long gray feathers.

20

There was *no way* I could work on the zombie movie after that. It was terrifying. I couldn't stop picturing Anna up there, perched like a bird, slipping forward and back on that high branch, holding on with both hands. Then disappearing.

It was clear that she really didn't remember it. And that made it even more frightening.

"I have to take Anna home," I told everyone.

"But we only have two days—" Marla started. "And Anna seems okay."

"I don't think so," I replied. "We'll have to regroup. Maybe tomorrow—"

Anna pulled another feather from behind her ear. She held it in front of her face and stared at it. "How did *that* get there?" she asked.

I put a hand on her shoulder and led her to the path. I could see the tire tracks from the fire engine in the dirt. But the truck was long gone. The firefighters thought we were playing a joke on them. But this was no joke.

"See you guys later," I called. I should have shown

the firefighters my video, I realized. In the confusion, I had forgotten all about it. But now it gave me an idea. A *major* idea. "Denzel, come with me," I said. "I need to talk to you."

"Did you really stop the video shoot because of me?" Anna asked.

"Don't worry about it," I said. "I have some new ideas for our movie."

She squinted at me. "New ideas?"

"Tell you later," I said.

Mom and Dad weren't home. They texted to say they were shopping in town. Anna hurried to her room. She wanted to see how Oggie was doing.

I pulled Denzel into the den. We sat down across from each other on the two leather armchairs by the fireplace.

Denzel leaned forward, clasping and unclasping his hands. I could see he was worried. "What are we going to do about your sister?" he said.

"Nothing," I replied.

He blinked. "Huh? Nothing?"

"The question is," I said, "what can Anna do for *us*?"

21

Denzel scratched his head. "I don't get it."

"Listen to me," I said. I leaned closer and spoke in a low voice. I wanted to make sure Anna couldn't hear me.

"Let's forget the zombie movie," I said. "It's garbage. I think—"

Denzel's face filled with surprise. "Garbage? But we're halfway finished," he started.

I raised a hand. "Just listen. Why should we do a fake zombie movie when I have a true-life horror story happening in my house?"

He thought for a second. "You're talking about the stuff with Anna?"

I nodded. "A weird bird in Anna's room bit her. And now she's starting to act more and more like a bird. I have some of it on video. And we can follow her and get more."

Denzel scrunched up his face. "You really think—?"

"How do you think she got up on that tree branch?" I said. "And how did she get down? She flew."

He stared at me and didn't reply.

"I recorded Anna sitting on the floor and chirping like a bird," I said. "And I watched her preening herself. And last night, she pecked at her food like a bird."

"No!" Denzel cried. "No way, Coop. Please tell me you're joking."

I raised my right hand in front of me. "I swear. It isn't a joke. That bird bite did something to her. And if we get it all on video, we'll have the most awesome horror movie ever—because it's totally true!"

Denzel jumped to his feet and began pacing back and forth. He had his hands in his pockets and his head down as he walked. I could see he was thinking hard.

Finally, he stopped in front of my dad's old grandfather clock in the corner. "Coop, this can't be happening," he murmured. "It's impossible."

"But it *is* happening," I replied. "You saw her up on that tree limb."

He thought some more. "Well . . . you have to tell your parents. You have to tell them what's happening to Anna."

"Of course," I said. "Of course, I'll tell them. But let's get our video recorded first. Let's get it all recorded. There's only a few days till the film festival deadline."

"But—but—" he sputtered.

"And then I'll tell Mom and Dad right away," I said.

"But . . . what if it's too late?" Denzel demanded.

"Too late for what?" I said. "They're scientists, remember? They'll know what to do."

He thought about that for a while. "You know, Coop," he said finally, "the joke may be on *you*."

I blinked. "Excuse me? What do you mean?"

"Well, Anna loves messing with your mind, right? Maybe she's doing the bird stuff to freak you out. Maybe it's her idea of a joke."

"It *is* freaking me out," I admitted. "But I don't think it's a joke, Denzel. I mean, you saw her up in the tree. That wasn't some kind of prank."

He shook his head. "I . . . I still don't believe it."

I climbed to my feet and motioned toward the doorway. "You need more proof? Okay. Let's go upstairs and see what she's doing now."

I took out my phone and got it ready to record. Then I led the way up the stairs. Denzel and I both tiptoed down the hall. I didn't want her to hear us coming.

Her bedroom door stood open. We crept up beside it. Denzel stood at one side of the doorway. I pressed up against the other side.

We both slowly poked our heads forward and peered in.

And we both screamed at once: "ANNA! STOP! DON'T!"

22

Anna's window was open. Her back was turned to us. She sat on the window ledge with her legs dangling outside.

Denzel and I both threw ourselves into the room. We bumped each other in the doorway, and I fell against the wall.

Denzel got to Anna first and grabbed her with both hands.

She uttered a startled squeak.

He lifted her under her arms and pulled her into the room.

She steadied herself on her feet and smiled at him. "What's up?" she asked.

Denzel was gasping for breath. I ran up beside him and turned to her. "Anna, you could have died!" I exploded.

She blinked a few times. Her smile didn't fade. "Died? How?"

"You . . . you . . . you looked like you were going to fall," I cried.

She scrunched up her face. "Fall? Fall from where?"

"You . . . you were on the window ledge," I stammered, pointing frantically.

"No, I wasn't," she said.

"We saw you," Denzel said, finally finding his voice. "You were on the ledge and—"

"No, I wasn't," Anna said. "What is your problem? Why did you grab me like that? I don't get the joke. Seriously."

"It isn't a joke," Denzel said. "What were you doing?"

"I was taking care of Oggie," Anna said. She walked over to the cage on the floor and dropped to her knees beside it. "Look at him. Doesn't he look better?"

"Better? How should I know? I've never seen him before," Denzel said. "What a weird bird. What is it?"

"We don't know," Anna said. "We can't identify it."

I stepped back and raised my phone. We had missed recording Anna on the window ledge. We were too scared at the time, but now I couldn't help thinking that it would have been a good scene. I pushed RECORD and started to film her conversation with Denzel.

"He had a sprained leg when I found him in the woods," Anna said. "But Mom and I put a splint on it, and now he's walking really well."

"Are you going to take him back to the woods?" Denzel asked.

Anna nodded. "When his leg is healed." She reached for the cage door and unlatched it. Then she pulled the door open.

"What are you doing?" I demanded.

"Oggie needs exercise," she answered.

70

The bird let out a squawk and strutted out of the cage, ruffling his wings up and down.

I kept the camera lens pointed at it. "Put him back, Anna," I said.

"Look how well he's walking," she said.

The bird squawked and flapped his wings.

"Put him back," I said again.

She made a face at me. "You're not the boss."

"That bird is dangerous," I said. "If he bites Denzel or me—"

"Are you recording this?" Anna demanded. "Why are you holding your phone up?"

"Never mind," I said. "Just put the bird back in the cage before he—"

I didn't finish my sentence.

The bird let out a shrill scream. Raised his wings high. Lifted off the floor—and flew out the open window.

SLAPPY HERE, EVERYONE.

Uh-oh. The bird just flew the coop.

But that weird bird is our villain, right? And now he's made his escape.

This could be a very short story! Hahaha!

Why do I have a feeling that Anna's troubles are just beginning? And why do I think Cooper's movie may turn out differently than he hopes?

Is it because I know the story? And I know the terrible things that happen next?

23

"NOOOOO!" Anna screamed. "I don't believe it!" She jumped to her feet and ran to the window. "My bird! Gone! NOOOOOO!"

Denzel spun around to face me. "Did you get that on video?"

I nodded. "Yeah. Got it."

Now what?

My mind was spinning. It was hard to think straight with Anna screaming her head off at the window.

Did we need the bird to finish our movie? Or could we just keep following Anna around, watching her strange behavior?

"He wasn't healed yet!" Anna screamed. She shook her fists at me. "How could you let him get away?"

"Me?" I said. "I'm not the one who left the window open."

"Yes, you are," Anna screamed. "I didn't open it!"

"Did you forget?" I said. "You were out there sitting on the window ledge!"

"Was not!" she cried. "You deliberately opened

the window. And now, everything is ruined. That bird wasn't ready—"

I heard a cough behind me and spun around.

Dad walked into the room. "Did somebody lose something?" he asked. He was carrying the bird in his arms.

Anna let out a scream. "Dad! How did you get him?"

"I was walking up the drive. He landed right in front of me. I think the splint on his leg kept him from really taking off."

Anna took the bird from his arms. "Oggie, why did you try to escape?" she asked him.

"Maybe he doesn't like the name Oggie," I said.

"Shut up, Coop," Anna muttered. She started to carry the bird to his cage. And as she passed me, the bird arched his head—and jabbed it forward, snapping at my shoulder.

"Oww!" I let out a cry and stumbled back.

Anna swung the bird away.

I rubbed my shoulder. "He . . . he almost bit me!" I cried.

Dad took my arm. He pushed up my sleeve and studied my shoulder. "He missed," Dad said. He grinned at me. "That bird doesn't like you."

A close call. I was lucky that time.

But guess what?

The *next* time, I wasn't so lucky.

24

Denzel stayed for lunch. He stopped me on the way to the kitchen. "Coop, listen," he whispered. "You really should tell your dad."

I whispered back. "Tell him what?"

"About your sister. What she's doing . . . it's too dangerous."

"You mean sitting out on the window ledge?" I said.

Denzel nodded. "And up in that tree? She could have broken her neck. You have to tell him. Seriously."

I let out a long sigh. "We're so close to finishing the video about her," I whispered. "I really want to enter it in the film festival."

"But—" Denzel started.

"Just a few more scenes," I said. "We'll keep a close eye on her. We'll make sure she doesn't do anything else dangerous."

Denzel shook his head. I could see that he didn't agree with me. But I can be stubborn sometimes, too. It runs in my family. And I knew a video of a girl turning into a bird would be a sensation. Because that's what was happening. I was sure of it.

I led the way to the table. Anna and Dad were already sitting down. Mom didn't come home after shopping. She had a tennis date with a friend.

Dad held a big pitcher and was filling glasses with his famous Power Juice. "Power Juice for breakfast and lunch," he said. "You'll feel the difference. Trust me."

Denzel placed his hand over his glass. "None for me, Mr. Klavan," he said. "I have a citrus allergy."

Is that really a thing?

"Listen to the birds tweeting out in the garden," Dad continued, tilting his ear toward the open window. "Isn't that the loveliest sound?"

I rolled my eyes. "Yeah. Lovely," I muttered.

Dad had this dreamy look on his face. "Can you imagine being as free as a bird? What a life. Flying everywhere. Spending your whole life outdoors in the fresh air."

"I think I'd catch a cold," I said.

Denzel laughed. "I don't think Coop agrees with you, Mr. Klavan."

"No one ever agrees with anyone in this family," Anna grumbled.

We all chewed away at our tuna sandwiches. Dad makes great tuna sandwiches, with tomato slices and tons of mayonnaise.

Across the table from us, Denzel and I both saw Anna's head bobbing up and down. She was pecking at her plate like a bird.

Dad was watching the birds out the kitchen window and didn't see her.

I reached for my phone to film her bird-pecking. But then Suzie jumped onto the table. Anna's cat is usually shy and very well behaved. But now Suzie had an intense look in her eye.

"Suzie, get down," I said.

But the cat ignored me and strode slowly across the table. She had her eyes fixed on Anna.

She walked silently, one step at a time. Her head was lowered as if she was stalking a mouse or something.

"Suzie—?" Anna cried. "What do you think you're doing?"

The cat took another step. Another.

Then she arched her back high. Her green eyes went wide. Her mouth opened, revealing her curved fangs.

A shrill screech escaped the cat's throat.

Anna raised both arms to shield herself. Too late.

The cat leaped onto Anna's face and dug her teeth deep into Anna's neck.

25

Anna uttered a shrill scream.

I shot to my feet, leaned over the table, and grabbed the cat in both hands. I gave a hard tug and pulled her off my sister.

"Anna, are you okay?!" Dad spun away from the window.

Anna wrapped her hands around her throat. "Owww," she choked out. Her eyes were wide in surprise.

Suzie struggled to break free from my grip. But I carried her out through the kitchen door and dropped her in the grass.

When I returned to the house, Dad was examining Anna's neck. "You're fine," he told her. "Hardly a scratch."

"But . . . but . . . why?" Anna stammered.

Denzel and I exchanged glances. We both knew why Suzie attacked my sister. The cat sensed what was happening. The cat realized that Anna was becoming a bird.

She attacked because that's what cats do to birds.

Why doesn't Dad realize what the cat has already figured out?

I was tempted to tell him the whole thing right then and there. Explain to him what Denzel and I had seen as we spied on Anna. Tell him that the evil bird was the cause of it.

But I held myself back.

Two more scenes, I told myself. *Just two more scenes, and the video will be complete.*

I knew I had something amazing on my phone. Something that would shock everyone who saw it. The video was going to be incredible. Maybe it would even win the Blue Ribbon award from the film festival.

Two more scenes. Then I'll tell Mom and Dad, I decided. *They'll know what to do. There will be plenty of time to save Anna.*

"Too bad about the cat attack," I told Denzel. It was later that afternoon, and we were in my room. "That was scary."

"Yeah, she could have been really hurt," Denzel said.

"No, too bad I didn't have a chance to record it," I said. "It was an awesome moment. It would have been great in our movie."

Denzel narrowed his eyes at me. "Maybe you're too psyched about your movie and forgetting your sister is in major trouble," he said.

"We're almost done," I said. "I just need one or two more scenes."

"What do you think she'll do next?" Denzel asked.

I didn't have to wonder for long.

I found out later that night.

26

I was sound asleep, dreaming about a soccer game.
It was a strange dream because I'm not on the soccer team at school, and I'm not into soccer at all,
really.

Denzel and Ezra were in the dream, too. They
were supposed to be on my team. But they both kept
kicking the ball at my face. I was yelling at them
and ducking my head when I woke up.

Mom says every dream has a meaning.

But *no way* could I figure out what that dream
meant.

It took me a few seconds to realize what had
awakened me.

I heard bumps and thumps in Anna's room next
door. A long scraping sound, like maybe she was
moving furniture.

I glanced at my bedside clock. 2:15 a.m.

"Why is she up?" I murmured to myself. "Is she
doing some weird bird thing?"

Yawning, I hurried into my jeans and T-shirt in
case Anna was going out. I tiptoed to my doorway.

It took a few seconds for my eyes to adjust to the total darkness in the hall.

Then Anna's door swung open and yellow light poured out from her room. I ducked back into my room so she wouldn't see me. I raised my phone and pushed RECORD.

My sister crept down the hall to the stairs. She passed right by my room, but I was hidden in the darkness. I stood as still as a statue and waited till she was out of sight. Then I followed her.

Where is she going in the middle of the night?

And what was she carrying? Was that a large trash bag?

I stopped halfway down the stairs. I kept the camera lens pointed at Anna as she carefully opened the front door. She slipped outside and silently pulled the door closed behind her.

I counted to ten. Then I opened the front door and followed her.

It was a cool, breezy night. The trees shivered in the wind, leaves clattering and whispering. A pale sliver of a moon floated high above the trees.

Anna walked in the street, holding the folded-up trash bag under one arm. I let her get a good head start. I didn't want her to turn around and see me. It would spoil the whole shoot.

The houses were all dark. Anna's shoes thudded on the pavement, the only sound except for the rush of wind through the trees.

She seems to be headed to the woods.

Yes. She turned at the dirt path that led into the

trees. Tree branches creaked and groaned in the gusts of cool wind. The leaves overhead whispered.

No. Please—not the woods! I thought. I don't like the woods in the daytime. I didn't want to be anywhere near them at night!

But I had no choice. I started to trot. I didn't want to lose her. I turned onto the narrow dirt path and squinted hard, trying to find her up ahead.

I could hear the scrape of her shoes on the dirt. But I couldn't see her. The leaves overhead blocked all moonlight. The tall, thick trees appeared to be black shadows against a blacker sky.

I had a sudden urge to call to her. *"Hey, Anna—?"* What if I caught up to her and simply asked what she was doing?

Then we could go home. In the middle of the night, every shadow, every soft sound, every slip of my shoes in the dirt was *terrifying* to me.

I felt a sting. Slapped a bug on the back of my neck.

Anna's footsteps stopped. I peered into the trees and saw her. She stood at the edge of the small clearing where we had been shooting the zombie video.

Why did she come back here?

I crept a little closer and hid behind a large tree trunk. Poking my head out, I watched her unfold the big trash bag. Then she bent down and began to pick things up from the ground.

In the dim light, I couldn't see what she was reaching for.

Anna worked quickly, scooping things up and dropping them into the large trash bag. I kept the phone trained on her. But I wasn't sure if the video would capture anything in this darkness.

Holding my breath, I crept a little closer. I had to know what she was collecting. Suddenly, my nose tingled. I felt a sneeze coming on.

No. Please, no.

I pinched my nose with my thumb and pointer finger. And held it tightly until the urge to sneeze passed.

I stood only a few feet away from her. But Anna was concentrating hard on her work. She had no idea I was standing there.

She didn't stop until the trash bag was bulging full. Then she stood up and took a few long breaths. She tied the top of the bag closed and began to drag it onto the dirt path.

I ducked behind a tree. She dragged it right past me. I could have reached out and touched her. Holding on to the cold tree trunk, I let her get a good head start again.

I knew where Anna was going. She was heading home.

Hanging far back, I watched her make her way into the street, dragging the trash bag at her side.

What was inside it? What did she plan to do?

I was shivering from the cold night air. But my forehead was drenched in sweat.

Maybe I was wrong to sneak out after Anna in the middle of the night. Maybe I should have told Mom and Dad.

But it was too late now.

I watched her disappear into the house. I waited

on the front stoop. Gave her plenty of time to get upstairs to her room.

What is she doing? What on earth is she doing?

Finally, I pushed open the front door and stepped inside. All was silent. No sound from Anna.

I tiptoed up the stairs. Walking quietly in the dark hall, I crept past my room. Holding my breath, I made my way to Anna's door and peered inside.

Her closet door was open. Bright yellow light spilled from the closet.

My mouth dropped open when she came into view.

And I saw exactly what she was doing.

27

She had dumped everything from the trash bag onto her closet floor. Squinting into the room, I saw a high pile of sticks and twigs and leaves and dirt.

Anna sat on her knees. Working quickly, she wove the sticks together and shoved dirt into the open spaces.

She was building a nest!

How did I feel watching her work? Horrified, of course. And also excited. This would be a major moment in my video.

I had my phone raised. I took a careful step into her room and started to film her nest-building. Anna was concentrating so hard on putting the twigs and sticks together, I knew I didn't have to worry about being seen.

As I recorded, the nest began to take shape. It looked like any bird nest you'd see in a tree, only bigger.

What did Anna plan to do with it? Did she plan to sleep in it?

I opened my mouth in a loud yawn.

Did she hear that?

No. She continued her work. But I yawned again. It was after three in the morning. My eyelids were heavy, and my whole body started to ache. I had to get some sleep.

I recorded a few more seconds of nest-building. Then I lowered the phone and backed out of her room. I dropped onto my bed and fell asleep with my clothes on.

The next morning, it was hard to shake myself awake. I kept blinking, trying to clear my head. I had the strong feeling that Anna's nest-building in the closet was all a dream.

Had I really followed her into the woods at two in the morning? Had I really watched her build a nest with twigs and sticks and dirt?

Did that really happen?

I grabbed my phone, brought up the video, and hit PLAY.

Yes. There she was down on her knees in her closet, the pile of twigs and sticks beside her on the floor. I didn't dream it. I had the whole thing on video.

I hurried down to breakfast. Mom and Dad were already at the table. "Sleepyhead, look what time it is," Dad said, motioning to the clock above the kitchen window.

"I . . . I didn't sleep well," I stammered.

Anna walked in and immediately started arguing with Mom about her cereal. "I don't want this." She sat down and pointed to the bowl. "It's too sweet."

"But you love this cereal," Mom said.

"Don't you have anything with seeds in it?" Anna asked.

Mom squinted at her. "Seeds?"

"Yeah. You know. Like . . . seeds."

"Why do you want seeds?" Mom demanded.

I could have answered that question. But I was curious to hear what Anna would say. Mom's phone buzzed before she could answer.

Mom grabbed it off the kitchen table and started to carry it away. "Sorry. I have to take this." She vanished into the other room.

I yawned. Then I poured myself a glass of Dad's Power Juice from the pitcher. I gazed across the table at my sister. "Anna," I said, "did you sleep well?"

She narrowed her eyes at me. "Why do you care?"

I shrugged. "Just asking."

"I slept okay," Anna said. "I don't really remember."

"You didn't go out or anything, did you?"

Her mouth dropped open. "Huh? Why would I go out?"

"Just asking," I said again.

Dad set down his coffee mug. "Cooper, stop questioning your sister. What's your problem this morning?"

"It's not *my* problem. It's *her* problem," I said.

I suddenly couldn't take it anymore. I couldn't hold it in. The feeling had been building and building inside me. I knew I *had* to tell Dad what was happening to Anna.

"Dad, I have to tell you something," I started.

He crunched on a mouthful of toast. Then he took a long sip of coffee. "What's up?"

"You know that bird upstairs? The one you brought home from the woods? Well—"

"You mean Oggie?" Anna interrupted. "What about Oggie?"

I ignored her and kept my eyes on Dad. "That bird bit Anna," I said. "And she's been acting strange ever since."

"Me? Acting strange?" Anna cried. "Why are you saying that, Cooper? You know it isn't true."

Dad patted Anna's hand. "Shhh. Give your brother a chance."

"A chance to tell lies about me?"

Dad stared her down.

"She's acting like a bird," I told him. "She's been sitting in her room chirping at the sky. At our zombie shoot in the woods, we found her on a high tree limb. We don't know how she got up there or down."

Dad turned to Anna. She shook her head no.

"Anna is afraid of the cat," I continued, "because the cat senses she's becoming a bird. Denzel and I caught her on her window ledge, perched there like a bird."

Anna propped her chin in her hands. "This is stupid," she muttered.

"It's not stupid. I'm worried about you," I said. "Dad, last night she sneaked out of the house. I followed her to the woods. She gathered a big bag of sticks and twigs. And she's building a nest in her closet upstairs."

"Ha ha," Anna let out a sarcastic laugh. "You're joking, right? I don't get the joke."

"I'm not joking. It's all true," I said.

88

I spotted something at the side of Anna's hair. I reached across the table and plucked it out. A long brown feather.

I held it up to Dad. "See?"

"What does that prove?" Anna cried. "I was handling Oggie this morning before breakfast. Big deal."

I twirled the feather in my fingers. "It's all true, Dad," I said. "I'm not making any of it up. I think she's growing feathers!"

He took another sip of coffee. Then he put the mug down and rubbed his cheek. He looked at me without blinking. He rubbed his cheek and stared for a long moment.

"Dad, say something," I urged. "Please. You do believe me—*don't* you?"

28

Dad gazed at me for another long moment. Then a smile crossed his face, and he chuckled. "That's very funny, Coop," he said.

"No!" I cried. "Dad—"

His grin spread wider, and he half closed his eyes. "I know I'm repeating myself. But . . . I wish we could *all* be birds," he said. "Wouldn't that be a great life? Out in the wild all day, nothing but fresh air and sunshine."

"But, Dad—" He had this dreamy look on his face. I wasn't even sure he heard me.

"What would that feel like?" he continued. "To take off and fly. To live high in the trees and fly for miles. And when you're hungry, dive into the water for fish."

He appeared to be in some kind of trance. I waved my hand in front of his face. "Dad, snap out of it."

The grin stayed on his face, but he focused his eyes on me.

"Dad," I started again. "Everything I told you about Anna—"

"He doesn't believe you," Anna interrupted. "He knows what you're saying is garbage."

I jumped to my feet. "It's *not* garbage!" I screamed. "It's all true! You've got to listen to me. That bird—it bit Anna, and she hasn't been the same."

Dad waved me back into my chair. "Take a breath, Coop. Your face is completely red."

"Tweet, tweet," Anna said sarcastically.

"Your mom and I are scientists," Dad said. "I've never heard of a bird bite that could lead to those kinds of symptoms. Sometimes an infection can be caused by a bite. But it would be impossible for a bite to start changing a person into a different kind of creature."

"But—but—" I sputtered.

"Just think about it for a second," Dad said. "Think how impossible the whole idea is."

I groaned. "Dad, I've thought about it for *days*. I know. I should have come to you and Mom sooner. But I'm telling you now—"

"TWEET, TWEET!" Anna leaned across the table and screamed in my face.

That made Dad laugh. "I think you're *both* bird-brains!" he cried.

I didn't laugh. I still had the feather from Anna's head in my fingers. "Okay," I said. "Okay. I know you think it's impossible," I told Dad. "And it does sound like it could never happen. But . . . I can prove it to you."

Dad's eyes went wide. "Prove it?"

I nodded. I reached for my phone to show Dad the video. But I had left it in my room.

I jumped up again. "Come to Anna's room. I'll show

you the nest she built. You'll see that I'm telling the truth."

Anna shook her head. "Stay out of my room," she snapped.

"Why?" I said. "Because you don't want Dad to see the nest in your closet?"

"No. Because it's a mess. I forgot to clean it up," she replied.

Dad took a last sip of coffee and climbed to his feet. "Don't worry about the mess," he said. "Let's take a quick look at your closet. You can prove that Cooper is making this whole weird story up."

Anna grumbled something under her breath.

I led the way to Anna's room. I was starting to feel better. It seriously upset me that Dad didn't believe what I was telling him. And he was grinning, when it was nothing to laugh about.

It was horrifying.

And now I could prove it, and Dad and Mom could figure out how to help Anna and get her back to herself.

We stepped into her room. The bed wasn't made and there were clothes scattered over the floor. But it wasn't totally messed up as Anna had claimed.

The closet door was closed. I trotted across the room. "The nest is right in front, Dad," I said.

Anna hung back at the doorway. "You're going to be sorry," she said.

"No, I'm not," I said. "I'm going to be glad that Dad will see the truth."

I grabbed the knob and pulled open the closet door.

29

"Huh?" A choking sound escaped my throat as I stared into the closet.

"Coop, I don't see a nest," Dad said, peering over my shoulder.

"Told you so," Anna said. She gave my back a shove.

The big plastic trash bag sat against the closet wall. It was round, bulging. Full.

I darted into the closet. I grabbed the top of the bag and pulled it open. "I told you!" I cried. "All the sticks and twigs." I turned to Dad. "I didn't make it up." I pulled out some sticks and raised them to him.

"You said Anna built a nest," Dad said.

"I know. But—"

Anna shoved me aside. She grabbed the sticks from my hands and dropped them back into the bag. "Do you want me to explain or not?"

"Yes. Explain," Dad said.

"These are for Oggie," she said. "I thought a nest would make him feel more comfortable."

Dad rubbed his cheek again. "But . . . when did you collect this wood?" he asked Anna.

"Last night," I said. "In the middle of the night. She sneaked out and—"

"I've been collecting it for days," Anna told him. "A little at a time. I planned to build the nest for him today."

"That's a lie!" I cried. "Dad, she's lying. I saw her last night. I followed her."

"You had to be dreaming," Anna said. "Or maybe that's one of the horror movie plots you've been making up."

Horror movie?

Whoa. Hold on a minute, folks.

My phone!

"Dad, I can prove everything I'm saying," I said. "I have it all on video."

Anna's mouth dropped open. "You *what*?"

"I've been secretly recording Anna," I said. "It's all my phone. You'll see it, Dad. You'll see Anna acting like a bird. Everything I said. It's all on video."

I made a face at Anna. "You lose. I have proof!"

Anna pressed her hands against her cheek. "I don't believe it," she murmured. "I don't believe you've been following me around and making a secret film."

She pounded my chest with both fists. "You're a spy! You're a dirty spy!"

I backed away. "Dad," I said. "I only did it because I was worried about her. It's very frightening. You'll see."

Dad narrowed his eyes at me. "Well, okay, Cooper. If you've got proof, let's see it. Go get your phone."

I crossed Anna's room to the hall.

"Dad, listen to me," I heard Anna plead. "What Coop did isn't right. Don't I have any privacy? Don't I have any rights? He can't make a secret video of me—can he?"

I didn't hear Dad's answer. I hurried into my room and crossed to my bedtable. That's where I'd left it this morning.

I leaned over to get it. "Weird." No phone there.

I fumbled over the collection of clutter on the bedtable. Some paperbacks and baseball cards and two sets of ear pods. Definitely no phone.

I turned and searched the bed. Did it fall into the bed this morning? No sign of it.

I crossed to my desk and gazed all around. Then I walked to the dresser. No sign of it there, either.

"My pocket!" I cried out loud. Of course. I must have stuffed it in my jeans pocket before going downstairs.

I slapped both pockets. No. No phone.

I walked the room slowly and searched the rug. Then I crossed back to the bedside table and went over it again.

"Coop—where are you?" I heard Dad shout from Anna's bedroom. "Why are you keeping us in suspense?"

I'M the one in suspense, I thought.

Where is my phone?

30

"I'll never find it if I panic," I told myself. I took a deep breath and held it.

My mind kept spinning. I got down on my hands and knees and searched under my bed. "Yes!" I grabbed for it. But it turned out to be a sneaker.

Suddenly, I knew where it was.

I must have brought it downstairs after all. I probably left it on the kitchen counter. I flew down the stairs, taking them two at a time. I burst into the kitchen, breathing hard.

I darted to the counter and—

No. No phone.

Struggling to catch my breath, I climbed back up the stairs and into my sister's room. Dad sat on the edge of the bed. Anna stood by the closet. They both looked up when I came slumping in.

"We're waiting to see your proof," Dad said.

I sighed. "You won't believe this. I can't find my phone. It's missing."

"No worries," Dad said. "Just call it."

Of course.

He handed me his phone. "It has to be here somewhere, Coop," he said.

I took Dad's phone and tapped in my phone number. I heard it start to ring instantly. I moved toward the sound and spotted it—behind Anna's laptop.

Squinting at it in surprise, I picked it up off the desk and stopped it from ringing. Then I spun around and raised it toward my sister.

"Anna—what is my phone doing on your desk?" I demanded. "How did my phone get in your room?"

She shrugged. "How should I know?" she said. "Think I took your phone? Well, I didn't."

"But . . . I didn't bring it in here and hide it behind your laptop," I argued.

"It wasn't hidden," Anna said. "It was sitting there in plain sight."

She crossed her arms in front of her. "What is your problem, Cooper? Do you really think I stole your phone and hid it from you?"

Dad jumped to his feet. He raised both hands. "Peace!" he cried. "Both of you—stop arguing.

"Coop, show us your videos," Dad said. "Let's see them. Show us your proof."

"Okay. Here they are," I said. I carried the phone over to Dad and Anna. They both gazed at the screen.

My hand trembled as I tapped the video icon. "I'm sorry I spied on you, Anna," I said. "But what's happening to you is very scary. I don't think you even realize—"

"No. I don't realize anything," she snapped. "Just stop talking and show us the videos."

"Okay. Here," I said. I raised the phone so they could see it clearly. And I pushed PLAY.

31

The screen remained black. Nothing happened.

The three of us stared in silence at the solid black rectangle, waiting for the video to begin.

"I must be at the end of it," I said. "I'll slide it to the beginning. No problem."

I tried to slide to the start.

Still nothing.

I tried it again. Nothing.

I pressed PLAY again and waited. Nothing but a black screen.

"What's up, Coop?" Dad asked.

"Something is messed up," I said. "A glitch. But I'll figure it out. Give me a second."

I went through all my videos. It had to be here. I went to the most recent one—and stared in shock.

"No way. This is impossible," I muttered.

The newest video was our zombie shoot in the woods. Marla had sent it to me from her phone.

The videos of Anna were gone.

Nowhere.

Nowhere.

Deleted?

My hand gripped the phone so tightly, it began to ache. I realized I had my jaw clenched tight. I suddenly felt as if my chest would explode in anger.

I tossed the phone to the bed and spun to Anna. "You—you—deleted my videos!" I screamed.

She backed away from me. "No way," she said calmly. "No way, Coop. I never touched your phone."

"Don't accuse your sister," Dad said. "Why would Anna delete your videos?"

"Because . . . because . . ." I sputtered. "She doesn't want you and Mom to know what's happening. She doesn't want you to see she's turning into a bird."

Anna laughed. She had this triumphant grin on her face. She stuck her elbows out and pretended to flap her wings.

"Tweet, tweet," she said.

32

"I *know* Anna deleted the videos," I said. "They didn't delete themselves. She must have seen me watching her last night."

Denzel shook his head. "Bad news."

We were at his house after school, sitting on the floor in his room, our backs against the bed. His mom had given us a big plate of fresh-baked chocolate chip cookies. It sat on the floor between us, untouched. Believe me, we didn't feel like eating.

"So our videos of Anna turning into a bird are gone," Denzel said, gazing down at the floor. "And our zombie movie is not even half-finished."

"Forget the movie," I muttered. "We'll have to enter something for the film festival *next* year."

Denzel kept his eyes down. "Yeah," he said. "I guess your sister is more important than any movie."

I thumped the floor with my fist. "Why didn't Dad believe me? Why did he believe Anna?"

"Because you had no proof?" Denzel replied. "Because your story is impossible to believe?"

"But you know I'm telling the truth about Anna,"

101

I said. "You saw it, too. If we *both* saw it, it has to be true, right?"

Denzel snickered. "What makes you think your dad will believe *me*? He'll think you and I cooked up the story together."

I punched the floor again. "How *could* she? How could she steal my phone and delete the videos?"

Denzel thought about it. "I guess she's desperate," he said finally. He turned to me. "If you were suddenly changing . . . I mean, if you started to act like a bird . . . wouldn't you do *anything* to keep it from people?"

"No way," I said. "I'd run to Mom and Dad. I'd tell them right away. I'd beg them for help."

"Well . . . you and your sister never agree on anything," Denzel said. "She's decided to keep it a secret."

Down the hall, in the living room, Denzel's younger twin sisters started to fight about something. They were both shrieking at each other. And I heard thumps and bumps.

"What if *your* sisters were turning into birds?" I said. "What would you do?"

"I'd be happy," he said. "It would be a lot quieter around here." He jumped up and shut his bedroom door.

"That's not funny," I said. "This is serious. We have to do something. How can I make my parents believe me?"

"Start filming her again?" he said.

"That will take too long," I said. "We have to act fast. You saw Anna up in that tree and on the window ledge. She keeps putting herself in danger and doesn't even realize it."

Denzel shrugged. "What can you and I do, Coop? Beats me. I'm totally stumped. We're not scientists. We don't know the antidote to that bird bite. Only your parents might know what to do. But if they don't believe you . . ."

The bird bite . . .

That weird bird . . .

My mind started to spin into overdrive.

I jumped to my feet and started to the bedroom door. "Denzel," I said, "I know the *first* thing I'm going to do. I have to get that bird out of the house! We're not safe with him there."

"No—don't!" Denzel blocked my way to the door. "Don't do it, Coop. It's too dangerous. If the bird bites *you* . . ."

I pushed him out of the way and hurried into the hall. "I have to do it," I said. "That's the first step. That bird has to go."

I didn't give him a chance to talk me out of it. I ran down the hall and out the front door.

If only I had listened to my friend . . .

33

My plan was to do it late at night.

Anna would be asleep, and maybe Oggie would be asleep, too.

I just had to sneak into her room and open the window. Then pull open the cage door, lift the bird, and toss him out into the night.

If I took the bird by surprise, the danger might not be great. But I knew Denzel was right. I had to make sure he didn't bite me.

Was I nervous? Yes. But I was also excited that I was finally doing something helpful. I couldn't wait for everyone to go to sleep.

Dinner seemed to stretch on forever. I couldn't think about anything but what I planned to do.

Mom asked me about the film festival. She had to ask me three times. I was lost in my own thoughts. I told her Denzel and I stopped working on the zombie movie. "We want to spend time doing something awesome for next year," I said.

Dad asked Anna if she was upset about not being a zombie. She mumbled something I didn't hear.

No one mentioned birds.

It was all I could think about. But I was grateful no one wanted to talk about the bird in Anna's room, or any other bird.

I hurried up to my room after dinner and tried to play some video games on my laptop. I wanted to take my mind off my bird plan. But it didn't work. I couldn't concentrate at all.

The night dragged on. Finally, around one in the morning, the house was dark and silent. I knew everyone had to be asleep.

I quickly prepared for invading Anna's room.

I pulled on a thick sweater. Over that, I wore my down winter parka with a wide wool scarf wrapped around my neck. I tugged a wool ski cap down over my face. And put on my heaviest leather gloves.

I was covered. Totally protected. *No way* the bird could get at me.

He could try to bite me. But he wasn't big enough or powerful enough to bite through all those layers.

My heart pounded in my chest. I took a deep breath. Then I crossed my room and stepped into the darkness of the hall. "Here goes," I murmured to myself.

You can do this, Coop. You can do this.

34

Anna's bedroom door squeaked as I pushed against it. I stopped with it half opened and listened. I could hear her soft breathing from her bed. She didn't wake up.

I slid the door open all the way and poked my head into the room. Silvery moonlight washed in from the window. Anna slept on her back with the covers pulled up to her chin.

Holding my breath, I tiptoed into the room and turned to the cage on the floor against the wall. Was the bird asleep?

No. I heard him cooing softly to himself. His feet thumped against the cage's metal floor.

I took a step toward him. Then another. My legs suddenly felt as if they each weighed two hundred pounds.

You can do this, Coop, I repeated to myself.

I pulled the leather gloves higher over my wrists. The wool ski cap and scarf itched like crazy, but I knew my face and neck were protected.

I was covered. Safe. No matter what the bird tried.

Yes, it was dangerous. But it had to be done. It was the first step to keeping the rest of us safe.

I stepped up to the cage and squatted down in front of the door. The bird tilted his head to one side and stared out at me through the thin metal bars. His wings fluttered softly at his sides. His dark eyes glowed in the silvery moonlight.

I don't care what you're thinking, I told him silently. *Your stay is over. You are out of here!*

My gloved hand trembled as I reached for the cage door handle. I gripped it tightly and slid the latch to the left. Then I slowly pulled the door open.

The bird uttered low sounds from deep in his throat. He fluttered his wings more rapidly. He tilted his head back.

I shoved both of my hands into the opening to block him from escaping. Then I shot my hands forward and wrapped my fingers around the bird's chest.

He let out a low squawk and struggled to bat my hands away with his wings.

But I held on tight and raised him from the cage.

Another soft squawk. Then the bird darted his head forward, snapping his beak.

He bit at my coat sleeve. Once. Twice. Snapped his head back. Then went for my gloved hand.

The bite didn't go through the leather. But I started to lose my grip. The bird slid heavily between my hands.

With a gasp, I tightened my fingers around him.

His wings beat furiously. He snapped at my coat sleeve again.

And opened his mouth in a shrill shriek.

"Hey—what's going on?"

Anna sat straight up in bed. She squinted at me, her eyes adjusting to the pale light. "Cooper? What are you doing in my room?" she cried.

The bird fluttered between my hands. I lurched to the window. *No way* I was going to let Anna stop me.

She cried out when she saw the bird in my hands. She dove out of bed and stumbled toward me, reaching out her arms.

"No! Stay back!" I cried. "He has to leave! He *has* to!"

"Let go of him! Let go!" Anna screamed. Her eyes wild, she leaped at me just as I swung my arms forward—and tossed the bird out the open window.

I watched him fly into the dark sky. Then I slammed the window shut.

"No!" Anna screamed. "Nooooo! How could you *do* that, you jerk? How *could* you? That was *my* bird!"

She grabbed my right hand and pulled off the glove.

Then she raised my hand to her face and bit deep into the skin.

35

"YAAAAIIII!"

I let out a cry and jerked my hand from her mouth. Pain shot up my arm. I ripped away the other glove and felt the back of my hand. Wet with blood.

"What did you do?" I screamed. "You . . . you bit me! Why—?"

Anna stumbled back and landed on the edge of her bed. "I . . . I . . . " She struggled to explain. But she couldn't seem to find the words.

"Why?" I repeated, holding my bleeding hand.

"I don't know!" she cried. "I guess I was just surprised. I mean . . . you burst into my room and tossed my bird out the window. What was I supposed to do?"

"*Not* bite me?" I said. "That would be one way to go. *Not* biting might be a better choice."

"I . . . I guess I was still asleep," Anna said. "I'm sorry. Can I get you a bandage or something?"

I didn't answer. I suddenly felt dizzy. This wasn't supposed to be the way it went down. I was fully protected so the evil bird couldn't bite me. And now, staring in horror at the bloody cut on the back of my hand, I thought that my sister could be just as dangerous.

Anna said something else, but I didn't hear her. A hundred thoughts raced through my head at once.

Am I going to be like Anna?

Will I start to chirp and grow feathers?

Am I going to turn into a bird now?

Should I run downstairs and tell Mom and Dad immediately? Is there anything they can do?

Is there anything ANYONE can do?

I staggered into the bathroom and ran cold water over the back of my hand. When I dried it off, the bleeding had stopped.

I stared at myself in the bathroom mirror. *The next time I looked, would I look like a bird?*

Sure I was scared. Who wouldn't be?

I stared at myself in the mirror until my panic started to fade.

"The bird didn't bite you," I told my reflection. "Only Anna bit you. That's not the same at all. Why should Anna have the power to turn you into a bird? You're going to be fine . . . perfectly fine."

I kept thinking that thought in bed, and before I knew it, I sank into a deep sleep. Sometime during the night, I had a very disturbing dream.

I was flying, flying high in the sky. I had wings, and I had them outstretched, and I was soaring in the clouds. I was surrounded by blue sky, and I could feel the cool wind in my face as I flew.

In the dream, I flew higher, climbing toward the clouds. And then suddenly I stopped—lowered my head and dove straight down.

A large body of blue-green water came into view. The water appeared to rise up to meet me. But I realized I was diving, diving into the water. I plunged into it without making a splash. Then I rose above the surface with a slim, silvery fish in my beak.

I woke up with a choked gasp. I sat straight up, instantly awake, my heart pounding.

It's happened. I'm a bird!

36

I jumped out of bed. Under my pajama shirt, my chest itched.

Feathers!

I tore open the pajama shirt and grabbed for them. No. Wait. Nothing but smooth skin.

I coughed and cleared my throat. Was I about to chirp like a bird?

I stood there in the center of the room and waited. No. I didn't feel like chirping.

Maybe I'm okay, I thought. *Maybe that bird dream was just a dream, and Anna's bite didn't change me at all.*

I crossed the fingers on both of my hands. *Coop, please be okay. Please be human.*

I lurched into the bathroom. I flashed on the light and stumbled to the mirror. Was my face covered in feathers? Had I grown a beak?

No. I blinked at my reflection.

I look the same.

I pumped my fists in the air. "I'm okay," I murmured. "I'm not turning into a bird. I'm still Cooper. Good old normal Cooper Klavan."

I rubbed my arms just to make sure they were smooth. I opened the pajama shirt and studied my chest in the mirror again.

No feathers.

"Wow." I breathed a long sigh of relief.

I hurried back to my room and pulled on a pair of jeans and a T-shirt. As I got dressed, I flashed back on the frightening scene in Anna's room last night.

I pictured myself creeping to the birdcage in the dark. And lifting that strange bird into my gloved hands. Once again, I pictured him stabbing his beak at me. Desperate to bite me.

But I won that battle. The bird went out the window.

Now Mom, Dad, and I were safe.

Yes, Anna bit my hand. But she was just frightened and startled. The bite didn't mean anything.

I'm fine. I'm perfectly fine.

My stomach grumbled. I had woken up hungry. I made my way downstairs to the kitchen. Was anyone else awake?

No. The kitchen was dark and silent.

I clicked on the light and crossed to the food cabinets. *I'll make myself a bowl of cereal,* I decided. I started to pull out the box of Frosted Mini-Wheats.

But then I had a different idea. I pushed the cereal box back into place. Then I opened the refrigerator. Squinting into the yellow light, it took me a few seconds to find what I was looking for.

"There they are."

The two cartons were still there at the back of the fridge. I grabbed one and lifted it out. I pulled the top open and peered inside.

The long brown bait worms were tangled around each other in a large clump of dirt. These were the worms we didn't use because our fishing trip had been cut short.

I reached two fingers into the carton and lifted out a long, wriggling worm. My stomach growled again. I usually wasn't this hungry first thing in the morning. I raised the worm in front of my face.

What am I doing?

The question flashed through my mind.

Why am I doing this?

I opened my mouth and lowered the worm onto my tongue. It had a tangy, metallic taste.

I didn't start to chew until I had shoved the whole worm into my mouth.

I tested the taste. Moist and meaty. Like spaghetti, but with a very special sauce.

I swallowed the next worm whole. Then I shoved two more into my mouth.

I'm eating bait worms. Why is this happening? Why am I enjoying it so much?

I should have been horrified. But I wasn't.

A worm poked out from my lips as I chewed. It tickled! I was pushing it back into my mouth when I heard a sound behind me.

I turned to see Anna, Mom, and Dad watching me from the kitchen doorway.

"What are you doing?" Mom asked.

"Uh . . . just having breakfast," I said.

37

Anna walked up to me and grabbed the white bait carton from my hand. She peered inside. "Empty. Didn't you save me any?"

"There's a whole other carton in the fridge," I said.

She tossed the empty carton back to me. That's when I saw the thick covering of brown and gray feathers up and down her arms.

"Dad, look—!" I rubbed my hand along Anna's feathers.

Anna jerked her arm away from me. "Let go." She uttered an angry bird squawk. Then she darted her head forward and pecked at my arm.

I backed up against the fridge. My chest started to itch again. I reached under my shirt and this time I felt something fuzzy on my skin.

Feathers! I was sprouting feathers, too!

"Mom! Dad! You have to believe me now!" I cried. "You have to help us. Look what that bird did! Look at Anna and me. We're turning into birds! You have to do something!"

To my shock, Mom and Dad both chuckled.

"It isn't funny!" I screamed. I lifted my shirt so

they could see the feathers sprouting on my chest. "Look what that bird did to us! Why are you two laughing?"

"I'll tell you why we're laughing," Mom said. "That bird didn't do this to you. Dad and I did!"

38

"Huh?"

"Excuse me?"

Anna and I both gasped.

"I . . . don't understand," I stammered.

"That bird didn't do anything to you," Dad said. "It's not from around here, and I don't know how it got in our woods. But it didn't have any powers. There's nothing special about it at all."

"Then . . . what?" I started. Short brown feathers were suddenly poking out of my arms. "What did this to us?"

"I did," Dad said, his eyes flashing excitedly. "Didn't you wonder about all the Power Juice I was making you drink every day? That was a very special formula. Our own mixture of bird DNA."

"Your dad and I have worked on that formula our whole careers," Mom said. "You have no idea how exciting this is. You two are our triumph. You are our victory."

"Our life's work is now a brilliant success!" Dad cried. He turned and hugged Mom. They both had tears in their eyes.

"Tweet! You . . . you mean you *experimented* on us?" I cried.

"On *all* of us!" Dad exclaimed.

Mom and Dad pulled up their sleeves.

"Oh, wow! Oh, I don't believe it!" I cried.

Anna and I shrieked our amazement as we saw the thick feathers covering their arms. Dad lowered his head so we could see the thick clump of feathers sprouting from his scalp.

"How many times have I told you how I envy the birds?" he said, grinning. "How many times have I said how I longed to live like a bird, flying free in the great outdoors?"

"And now we can," Mom said. She tossed back her head and crowed. Dad joined her, and they flapped their arms and crowed some more.

"My life's dream," Dad said when they finally finished. "The Power Juice formula worked. I have to admit—we were a little worried about you. Your feathers took a bit longer to grow. But now we can all live in the trees and fish for food in the pond."

"Let's go!" Mom cried.

Dad opened the kitchen window. We all held hands for a moment and took a deep breath. Then we flapped our feathered arms and flew off over the trees.

EPILOGUE FROM SLAPPY

Hahaha. I *love* a happy ending—don't you?

As I always say, the family that flies together *eats* flies together! Or maybe worms. Haha.

I wish I could grow feathers. I'd use them to *tickle* people until they screamed! Hahaha.

Well, I don't want you to worry, my Fine Feathered Friends. I'll be back soon with another Goosebumps story.

Remember, this is *SlappyWorld*.

You only *scream* in it!

PARTY TIME . . . OR ELSE!

SLAPPYWORLD #19:
FRIIIGHT NIGHT

Read on for a preview!

1

Let's say you were an ant, and you lived with your ant family in a little dirt hole under someone's porch. Then one day, someone dug up the dirt hole and carried it in a truck a few hundred miles and dropped it in the middle of the world's biggest ant farm.

How would you feel?

Well, you probably can't answer that question—unless you're an ant. I'm trying to describe how I feel, having moved from Little Hills Village, New Hampshire, to Great Newton, Massachusetts. I don't mean that Little Hills Village is a dirt hole. It's just tiny compared to Great Newton, see.

I'm Kelly Crosby. I'm twelve. And you can probably tell that I'm a little messed up by my family's move. In the middle of the school year. To a town where I don't have a single friend or even know anyone.

I was in the back seat of our car, on my way to my first day of school, and I started to text my friend Charlene Morse back home. But I decided I had too much to say, so I called her instead.

"Charlene, if I was an ant, I'd say, 'Someone please step on me!' I groaned.

She was silent for a moment. Then she said, "I hate ants. Why are you talking about ants?"

"Because I feel like one," I said. "And because there were ants in the kitchen when we moved in. Mom put down so many ant traps, you can't walk barefoot in there."

"Well, stop talking about them," she said. "What's new?"

"Huh? What's new? *Everything* is new," I replied.

"Kelly, you don't sound happy," Charlene said.

"Is an ant happy in the ocean?" I exclaimed.

She sighed. "Kelly, I'm going to hang up now. If you say the word *ant* one more time . . ."

"We have mosquitos, too," I said. "I-I guess I miss Little Hills Village. Tell me what's up? What's going on there?"

"You know what's going on here," she replied. "Nothing. It's so boring here—"

"I like boring," I said.

"Okay, Kelly. I'll tell you the big news. Two dogs got into a dogfight on the lower school playground last Friday. That's the big news."

"Who won?" I asked.

We both laughed.

I think Charlene and I are good friends because we have the same sense of humor. We make the same jokes, and we both laugh at the same things.

But then she turned serious. "Listen to me. You're so lucky. You'll love Adams Prep. A big school will be so much more exciting."

"Who likes exciting?" I said.

"Stop it," she snapped. "I'm totally jealous of you, Kelly. New kids. A big new school. Just think. You can be a new person with a new personality."

"Huh?" I replied. "What's wrong with my old personality?"

"I didn't know you *had* one!" she joked.

Or, maybe it was a joke.

"Did you buy new clothes for the new school?" Charlene asked. "Did you throw away that *Puppy Pals* T-shirt?"

"You're not funny," I said. "You know I wore that shirt ironically."

"I hope you burned that other shirt you thought was such a riot."

"Which one?" I asked. "The one that said *Don't Read This Shirt?* Everyone laughed at that T-shirt."

"Those were sympathy laughs," Charlene said. "Let's be honest. You were kind of a wimp here. Now you have a chance to try a bold new personality. How lucky to be able to start over!"

Mom pulled the car to the curb. I gazed out at the tall, redbrick Adams Prep school building. Groups of kids were hurrying to the wide front entrance.

The school was huge.

"Gotta go," I told Charlene. "We're here."

"Good luck," she said.

"Does an ant need good luck in a forest?" I said.

Mom squinted at me. "Stop talking about ants."

A big guy bumped me from behind as I stepped into the front hall. I guess I was moving too slowly. The noise of lockers slamming and kids shouting and laughing rang against the tile walls. There were more kids in the front hall than I had ever seen in my entire school.

Two guys were playing keep-away, tossing another guy's backpack across the hall. Two girls in red-and-blue cheerleader outfits were practicing a cheer at the top of their lungs.

A tall kid in blue shades with a blue cap tilted over his face leaned against a locker, playing a small silver harmonica.

A girl sailed into the hall on a skateboard. Kids dodged out of her way.

"This is a fun place," I muttered to myself. *I'm going to like it here. I'll get used to it, and I'll start to love it.*

But I already had a problem. I didn't know how to find my classroom.

My school in Little Hills Village was a low, flat building. It didn't take long to walk from one end to the other.

But the halls at Adams Prep were at least half a mile long. The building was three floors, not one. I saw an elevator at the back wall. A sign next to it read: TEACHERS AND STAFF ONLY.

I shifted the backpack on my shoulders. It was mostly empty. I hadn't received any textbooks or anything yet. I ducked as a red Frisbee flew over my head.

I turned to the kid who threw it. "Ms. Waxman's class?" I asked.

"Downstairs."

"But where are the stairs?"

He didn't hear me. He had chased after his friend, the other Frisbee player.

Kelly, you can find the stairs, I told myself.

Sure, I felt a little overwhelmed by the crowd of kids and the noise. I get overwhelmed sometimes. Mom says I'm *sensitive*. I think that's her polite way of saying I'm a wimp.

But I'm not helpless. And just because I was used to a tiny village and a tiny school didn't mean I couldn't handle something new.

Charlene's words rang in my ears: "Now you have a chance to try a bold new personality."

So I gritted my teeth, pushed my shoulders forward, and made my way through the crowd. The hall branched off into two long corridors, and I took the one on the left. I passed the principal's office. Through the office window I saw a mob of kids and teachers lined up at the front desk.

I passed some classrooms. Then I stopped at a red painted wooden door. I pulled it open and saw a metal stairway that led down.

"That wasn't so hard, Kelly," I scolded myself.

I stepped into a dimly lit stairwell. The air felt warm and it smelled like a basement, kind of musty and sour. I listened for a moment. Silence.

I hesitated. Why wasn't anyone else on the stairs? Then I let go of the door and started down.

I was halfway to the bottom when I heard a deep growl.

I stopped. And listened. Was it an animal growl?

Yes. I heard another one, low and angry. A dog?

Another rumbling growl sent a chill down my back. I turned, grabbed the banister, and pulled myself back up the stairs.

I stepped into the hall and shut the red door behind me.

What had I heard? What kind of animal was down there?

Why was there some kind of animal in the basement of this school?

3

I leaned against the door and waited for my heart to stop pounding. Everyone was hurrying to their classrooms. A buzzer went off above my head. I jumped about a mile. I guessed that was the morning bell.

I saw a kid across the hall pulling books from an open locker. "Hey," I called to him and headed over.

He had curly, copper-colored hair and a face full of freckles. He closed his locker door and turned to me. "What's up?"

"I-I'm just starting today," I stammered. "Do you know where Ms. Waxman's classroom is?"

He swung his backpack over his shoulders. "I'm in Waxman's class," he said. "Follow me."

"Awesome," I said. "I'm new. I . . . got kinda lost."

He snickered. "I've been here for three years, and I still get turned around." He studied me for a moment. "Where you from?"

"Little Hills Village."

He snickered again. "Is that a real place? It sounds made up."

"It's very tiny," I said. "You can find it on Google Maps, but you have to really zoom in to see it."

That made him laugh. His blue eyes flashed. He had a friendly laugh.

"I'm Gordon Willey," he said. "A lot of kids call me Gordo, and I hate it."

"Okay, Gordo," I said. I couldn't resist. It made him laugh again. I told him my name.

I thought maybe we could be friends.

The hall was emptying out. A second buzzer rang, echoing down the long corridor. I followed him up a wide stairway.

"I can help you find things," he said. "Like, there's no boys' room on the first floor. You have to hold it in till you get to the second floor."

"Good to know," I said.

"And the lunchroom is on three," he said. "Weird, huh?"

He stopped at a room marked 104-B. "Here you go," he said. "Waxman's room. You'll like her. She's seriously nice."

"Awesome," I said. "Some kid told me Ms. Waxman's classroom was downstairs."

"They were playing a joke on you. There aren't any classes down there. It's just the basement."

I started to thank him, but he interrupted me. "Hey, you're lucky, Kelly. You got here just in time for Friiight Night."

"Huh?" I wasn't sure I heard him right. "Friiight Night? What's that?"

But he was already in the room, and I didn't get an answer.

Ms. Waxman was standing with two girls behind her desk. They were looking at something on an iPhone. "That's rad," she said to the girls. "Don't tell your parents I said so."

She turned as I walked in. "The new kid!" she exclaimed.

I nodded and took a few steps toward her.

"Know how I figured that out?" she asked. "Because I've never seen you before."

I laughed. She was making a joke. "You're a good detective," I said.

She was young, with straight black hair cut very short, dark eyes, and a nice smile. I saw a tattoo of a red heart on her wrist. Teachers at my old school wouldn't dare have tattoos.

She blew a metal whistle and everyone got quiet. "I used to be a soccer coach," she explained. "And I just can't bear to give up my whistle."

She's funny, I thought. *I think I'm going to like her.*

Ms. Waxman leaned over her desk and raised a sheet of paper. "You're Kelly Crosby," she said. "Hey, everyone, this is Kelly Crosby," she announced. "Where are you from, Kelly?"

"Little Hills Village," I said.

She nodded. "Oh yes. I drove through there once. But I sneezed and I missed it."

A few kids laughed.

"It's very small," I said. "And my school was small, too."

"I'll bet it was so small, your shadow had to wait outside!" She grinned, enjoying the kids' laughter.

I never had a comedian for a teacher before, I thought.

"Well, let's all welcome Kelly to Adams Prep," she said. "And be nice to him. He probably finds you all pretty scary. I know *I* find you scary!"

I could feel my face turning red. The kids were all staring at me, studying me, I guess. It was too much attention, and I'm an easy blusher.

Ms. Waxman pointed to a chair-desk combo by the window near the back of the room. "There's an empty desk, Kelly," she said. "Why don't you take it?"

I nodded and started for the desk.

"You have a lot of catching up to do," she called after me. "Especially with Friiight Night coming so soon."

I slid into the chair and dropped my backpack to the floor. "What is Friiight Night?" I asked.

But she had turned to talk to a girl in the front row and didn't hear me.

I gazed around the room, searching for Gordon. He was near the back against the other wall. He had his head down, concentrating on something in a blue notebook.

Ms. Waxman perched on the edge of her desk. "I'm going to pass out a Tournament Quiz in a moment," she said. "Or should I just pass out?"

She waited for the laugh.

Then she continued. "First, I have an announcement to make. Our class has been named Activities Committee for Friiight Night."

A few kids gasped. A few cried out in surprise. I couldn't tell if it was good news or bad.

"You know what that means," the teacher continued. "We have to think of some fun activities and entertainment for everyone." She gazed around the class. "I can see you're already thinking. Well . . . that's your homework assignment. Make a list of five things that would be good for Friiight Night."

I raised my hand. I *had* to find out what Friiight Night was. How could I do the homework assignment if I didn't know what it was?

But Ms. Waxman didn't see me. She had turned away again and picked up a stack of papers from her desk. Then she began walking through the rows of desks, handing them out.

She stopped at my desk. "Listen, Kelly," she said, "I know you're new. But you have to try your very best on the Tournament Quizzes."

"Seriously—?" I started.

Her eyes narrowed and her smile faded. "There will be five more quizzes, and you have to do well. You don't want to come in last in the class," she said. "You don't want to be the monster's date on Friiight Night."

Huh? The monster's date?

"Friiight Night? What's Friiight Night?" I demanded.

She set the paper down on my desk. "Start the quiz," she said. "You're going to need as much time as possible."

"But—"

"You can ask one of the kids to tell you about Friiight Night later," she said. "Good luck."

Why was everyone wishing me good luck today?

Saturday, I did a FaceTime call with Charlene back home. "Do you miss me?" I asked.

"Not really," she said.

I think she was joking. I told you, we have the same sense of humor.

"I have a lot of new friends who are cooler than you," she said.

"Name six," I replied.

She laughed.

"I have kind of a new friend," I said. "His name is Gordon. But it's hard to make friends when you come in the middle of the year. Everyone already knows everyone."

"I don't feel sorry for you, Kelly," Charlene said. "It's so boring here. I keep wishing for those two dogs to have another fight on the playground."

"I made a plan to go bowling with Gordon next Saturday," I said.

"Huh? You? Bowling? Will you have someone help you lift the bowling ball?"

"Haha," I said. "I always wanted to try it. Which

was impossible since there's no bowling alley in Little Hills Village."

"Tell me about it."

"I passed a really cool one a few blocks from school," I said. "It had this huge neon sign with three bowling balls flying in the air."

"Too much excitement," Charlene said. Sometimes she can be seriously sarcastic.

I had my phone facing me, propped against my laptop. I sat in my desk chair and juggled three balls while I talked to Charlene. My Uncle Pete was a circus clown, and he taught me how to juggle when I was five.

"Are you showing off your one talent again?" Charlene asked.

"You're jealous," I said. I began juggling the balls faster.

"I'm jealous because you're in a big, new school," she said. "And I have Mr. Potner for the second year in a row.

"Potner rules," I said.

Then I decided to change the subject and tell her what I had really called about. "The school has this thing coming up real soon. It's called Friiight Night. With three I's."

"Maybe you need three eyes to go to it," Charlene said. "What is it? Some kind of party?"

"I guess," I said. "But I can't get anyone to tell me what it is. I just know it's a big deal. They keep talking about it. And every time I ask what it is, they say they'll tell me about it later, but then they don't."

"Maybe it's like a Halloween party," Charlene suggested. "Everyone dresses up and tries to be scary."

"Maybe," I said. "The teacher said there's a monster. Maybe that's what she meant."

Talking to Charlene was already making me feel better. I was wondering what that monster thing was all about. It was probably a scary party with scary costumes. That made sense.

I tossed one of the balls too high, missed it, and it bounced onto the floor. I picked it up and started juggling again, more carefully.

"My class is in charge of activities," I told Charlene. "We're supposed to think some up. But how can I when I don't really know that Friiight Night is?"

"Maybe you could give juggling lessons," she replied. "That could be fun."

"I don't know," I said. "I guess—"

I stopped because I heard a knock on the front door. I jumped up and crossed to my bedroom window. Gazing down at our front stoop, I saw Gordon and two other kids.

"Talk later," I told Charlene. "Gotta go."

I ended the call and tucked the phone into my jeans pocket. Then I hurried to the front door. I pulled it open to see Gordon with a girl and another boy behind him. Gordon lived around the corner. I'd seen him riding his bike down my street. All three of them were in my class.

"Hey, what's up?" I said.

"Come with us, Kelly," Gordon said. He grabbed my arm and started to pull me from the doorway.

"What? Where are we going?" I demanded.

"You've been in school a week," he said. "It's time for you to meet the monster."

I closed the door behind me, and we started to walk
toward school. It was late afternoon and warm and
sunny. Someone in the neighborhood was having
a barbecue. A gust of smoke carried the aroma of
hamburgers.

No one spoke. They were walking quickly, taking long strides, and I had to hurry to catch up.
"Gordon." I tapped his shoulder. "It's Saturday. Isn't
the school closed on Saturday?"

"No worries," he said. "You need to come with us
today."

"Is this some kind of Adams Prep tradition?" I
asked.

He shook his head. "It's not a tradition," he
answered. "It's a school *rule*."

"You meet the monster after your first week of
school," the girl said. Her name was Penny May. She
was nice. She had helped me find the art room last
week when I was walking around in circles.

She stepped up beside me as we crossed to the
next block. "Kelly, are you scared?"

"Huh?" I squinted at her. "Should I be scared?" I suddenly remembered the growls in the basement. "Seriously. Should I be scared?"

No one answered. I felt a chill at the back of my neck.

Gordon waved to an SUV that slowly rolled past, filled with kids I recognized from school. "Just remember, Kelly, don't show any fear."

"Don't shake or whimper or anything," Penny May said.

I choked a little "Now you're starting to scare me."

Gordon stopped walking and turned to me. "No worries. Adams has the best school monster in the state."

"Yeah," Kwame, the boy behind me spoke up. "Those snobs at Madison Academy are always bragging about their monster," he said. "But Skwerm rules!"

I stared at him. "Skwerm?"

"What's a Skwerm?" I demanded.

"You'll see," Kwame said.

I followed them into the school through one of the side entrances. The hall must have just been washed. It smelled of strong detergent.

There was no one around. Our shoes thudded loudly in the empty hall as we made our way toward the back. Gordon stopped at the red door that led to the basement.

"Hey, wait. Someone tell me what we're doing," I said.

No one answered me.

"Skwerm totally slaps!" Gordon said. "He can beat Burrrph any day of the week."

"I bet Skwerm can beat Burrrph with his claws tied behind his back," Penny May added.

"Skwerm could *eat* Burrrph!" Kwame exclaimed. "Wouldn't that be awesome?"

The three of them burst out laughing.

I watched them, thinking hard. Then I *finally* figured out what was going on.

"I get it," I said. "Oh, wow. I finally get it."

They stared at me.

"This is a joke you play on all the new kids," I said. "Okay. Okay. You really had me going for a while. But now I get it."

Gordon shook his head and frowned at me. "Joke? What makes you think it's a joke?"

"We don't joke about Skwerm," Kwame said.

Gordon pulled open the red door.

I gulped loudly when I heard the angry animal growl floating up from down the stairs. I felt another chill at the back of my neck. "Uh . . . guys . . . what *is* that?" I uttered.

Gordon held the door open and gave me a push into the stairwell. "Let's go, Kelly. Down the stairs. I hope Skwerm likes you."

SLAPPY HERE, EVERYONE.

So Kelly is about to meet Skwerm. Think they'll become best friends?

I don't think so.

Meanwhile, back in Little Hills Village, Kelly's friend Charlene is worried about him.

Guess what, folks? She has *good reason* to be worried! Hahaha!

About the Author

R.L. Stine says he gets to scare people all over the world. So far, his books have sold more than 400 million copies, making him one of the most popular children's authors in history. The Goosebumps series has more than 150 titles and has inspired a TV series and two motion pictures. R.L. himself is a character in the movies! He has also written the teen series Fear Street, and the Mostly Ghostly and Nightmare Room series. He is currently writing a series of graphic novels entitled Just Beyond. R.L. Stine lives in New York City with his wife, Jane, an editor and publisher. You can learn more about him at rlstine.com.

Catch the
MOST WANTED
Goosebumps® villains
UNDEAD OR ALIVE!

SPECIAL EDITIONS

■ SCHOLASTIC
scholastic.com/goosebumps

GBMW42

REVENGE OF THE LIVING DUMMY
R.L. STINE

CREEP FROM THE DEEP
R.L. STINE

MONSTER BLOOD FOR BREAKFAST!
R.L. STINE

THE SCREAM OF THE HAUNTED MASK
R.L. STINE

DR. MANIAC VS. ROBBY SCHWARTZ
R.L. STINE

WHO'S YOUR MUMMY?
R.L. STINE

MY FRIENDS CALL ME MONSTER
R.L. STINE

SAY CHEESE - AND DIE SCREAMING!
R.L. STINE

WELCOME TO CAMP SLITHER
R.L. STINE

THE SCARIEST PLACE ON EARTH!

The Original Bone-Chilling Series

—with Exclusive Author Interviews!

NIGHT of the LIVING DUMMY
R.L. STINE
SCHOLASTIC

DEEP TROUBLE
R.L. STINE
SCHOLASTIC

MONSTER BLOOD
R.L. STINE
SCHOLASTIC

The HAUNTED MASK
R.L. STINE
SCHOLASTIC

ONE DAY at HORRORLAND
R.L. STINE
SCHOLASTIC

The CURSE OF the MUMMY'S TOMB
R.L. STINE
SCHOLASTIC

BE CAREFUL WHAT YOU WISH FOR
R.L. STINE
SCHOLASTIC

SAY CHEESE and DIE!
R.L. STINE
SCHOLASTIC

The HORROR at CAMP JELLYJAM
R.L. STINE
SCHOLASTIC

HOW I GOT MY SHRUNKEN HEAD
R.L. STINE
SCHOLASTIC

SCHOLASTIC

www.scholastic.com/goosebumps

GBCL22

R.L. Stine's Fright Fest!
Now with Splat Stats and More!

GET YOUR HANDS ON THEM BEFORE THEY GET THEIR HANDS ON YOU!

ALL 62 ORIGINAL
Goosebumps
AVAILABLE
IN EBOOK!

SCHOLASTIC
scholastic.com

GBCLRP2

CONTINUE THE FRIGHT
AT THE GOOSEBUMPS SITE
scholastic.com/goosebumps

FANS OF GOOSEBUMPS CAN:

- PLAY THE GHOULISH GAME:
  GOOSEBUMPS: SLAPPY'S DROP DEAD HOUSE

- LEARN ABOUT NEW BOOKS AND TERRIFYING CLASSICS

- TAKE A QUIZ AND LEARN WHICH TYPE OF MONSTER YOU ARE!

- LEARN ABOUT THE AUTHOR WHO STARTED IT ALL: R.L. STINE

SCHOLASTIC

GBWEB2019